MAGENTA
SALVATION

MAGENTA
SALVATION

sequel to
Virtue Inverted
and
Amazon Expedient

by

Piers Anthony
and
Kenneth Kelly

Magenta Salvation
Copyright © 2019 by Piers Anthony and Kenneth Kelly

Cover Art & Design:
Editor-in-Chief: Kristi King-Morgan

Printed in the United States of America

ISBN: 978-1-947381-15-5

www.dreamingbigpublications.com

Prologue

The Pawben didn't know how long he'd been asleep when he awoke to the sun blinding his eyes. Sitting up, he realized he was sitting on a grassy knoll which sloped down to a river that looked an awful lot like the Gant River of his childhood. A cool breeze wafted through the trees behind him, tousling his snow-white hair and beard. He took a deep breath. The setting was invigorating; he could almost feel his youth returning to him. He crawled down to the riverbank and leaned over the gently rolling stream to get a drink when he gasped at his reflection. He looked as if he were barely 16, with long flowing hair and, most importantly, no scar disfiguring his face.

"Hey, silly goose," a voice said behind him.

Could it be…? Yes, it was. Virtue stood at the edge of the forest behind him, an opalescent dress draping her curvaceous body.

"Get over here," she commanded.

Tears streaming down his now restored cheeks, Benny dashed into Virtue's embrace. Together they stood, each nuzzling their mouths in the crook of the other's neck. Benny didn't want to let go, but finally his wife pushed him back.

"Your time here is short, for now, and as much as I'd like, I can't afford to waste that time cuddling." She smiled and Benny's heart soared.

"How?" Benny asked.

"Let's just say an old friend named Search gave us this reunion in return for a few errands he had me run. The others wanted to come, too, but we figured this would be better."

Benny looked down at himself and noticed his body begin to age. The scar had returned, and his hair and beard were growing and beginning to transform back into the gray mane they had been.

"Let me stay, I beg of you!"

"I'm not the one who makes that decision, love. You know that." Virtue held him close once again.

"I've traversed hundreds of worlds...diverted wars, made and lost friends, and suffered hardships no creature should ever endure. My time is almost spent, I can feel it. I have nothing more left in me."

"Do you forget the task you took from Dale's son? Have you forgotten the child, Aldwin Beranger?" Virtue teasingly slapped the old man's face.

"It's not that I've forgotten him, Virtue. My bones are brittle, my once great magic is nearly spent, and the pain of staying away from you and the others haunts my mind."

"Don't fret, love. The Protector knows how you long to be reunited with me...with all of us...but you cannot abandon the boy yet."

"But I've already arranged for Toadstool to take care of the boy if..."

"I'm glad you've made such a trusting friendship with Toadstool, but the task was given to you, Benny. Not him."

"Please..." Pawben pleaded, now on his knees. He buried his face into Virtue's stomach. She ran her fingers through his coarse, white hair, making him shiver in joy and anguish.

"You have one last adventure you must see through...one last task. One you and Aldwin must do together. When it is finished, the gauntlet will be passed on to him, and he will continue your work, and that of his forefathers." Virtue leaned over, kissing the old man passionately one final time.

"I can't..." Pawben sobbed.

Virtue's playful laughter filled his ears as everything faded to black. "You always made mountains out of molehills," She placed her hand on his cheek one last time. "It won't be long, Ben. Trust me on this one."

The Pawben awoke as he fell face-first off the edge of the couch. He banged his nose on the hardwood floor, causing a thin stream of blood to trickle onto the floor as he rose to all fours. He was dizzy, breathing in short, hard gasps that sounded as if he were trying to stifle a cry. He finally arose, looking around him before remembering where he'd spent the night. Wet with sweat, he tore off his robes until he wore nothing but his skid-marked underpants. Pawben looked down at his wrinkled body. *Not bad for 200 years,* he thought. Looking around in the darkness, he saw the faint glow of candlelight illuminating the stairs to the second floor, and upon grabbing his staff, staggered up them to find Toadstool in his small library, reading from a book and puffing on a crude cigar.

"Thought you quit those things," Pawben said, startling Toadstool and causing the tortoise to drop both book and cigar on the floor.

"You nearly scared me out of my shell!" He picked up his cigar and continued puffing as he resumed his reading.

Pawben looked over at the other end of the room and saw the little boy, Aldwin, asleep on Toadstool's bed.

"Mind if I join you?" Pawben pulled up a chair across from Toadstool. "Give me one of those."

Toadstool reached into a small jar on the table beside him, pulled out a cigar, and handed it to Pawben. The old man bit the tip off the head, raised his right forefinger to the foot of the cigar, and in an instant Pawben was puffing thick white smoke.

"Parlor tricks," Toadstool stated.

"That's about the only thing that keeps me from forgetting my magic altogether."

The whole time they sat together, Toadstool never looked up from his book. "What's bothering you?" he asked.

"Why do you ask that?"

"Cuz I heard you downstairs, whimpering like a stuck pig." His eyes looked up at the old human across from him. "And you muttering some garbage about pawning that boy off on me."

For a second, Pawben thought Toadstool was angry, but the tortoise winked at him, chuckled, and set down the book next to the jar of cigars.

Pawben accidentally inhaled too much smoke and nearly fell out of his chair as a riotous coughing fit ensued. He held the cigar up in front of him and winced. "I prefer my pipe, thank you," he said. He stuck it back in his mouth and leaned back in his chair.

"You didn't answer my question...what's bothering you?" Toadstool pressed the question.

"Oh, just a dream I had."

"A nightmare?"

"No, it was good...in a way...I was with someone I used to know." Pawben looked down at his long, dirty toenails.

"Virtue?" Toadstool asked, grinning.

"How did you...?"

"You were saying her name over and over and..."

"Ok, I get it," Pawben took a long draw on his cigar. "Yes, it was her. I haven't communicated with her in quite some time. It was pleasant, but a bit unsettling when I realized I wasn't staying with her. I'm surprised my vision was with her and not my other wives."

"Because you loved her most," Toadstool teased.

"No...I loved them all," Pawben was sincere, "but she was first. Perhaps that's why Search chose to reunite us for that brief respite."

"Well, what *did* Virtue say, if you don't mind me asking?"

"Something about one last journey the boy and I were going to take in the near future...something about passing my work on to him." Pawben sighed, spewing smoke out his mouth and nostrils.

"I thought you were trying to prevent Aldwin from following in y'all's footsteps?" *Why won't you wipe that stupid smirk off your face?* Pawben thought as Toadstool finished his sentence.

"I am…but it would appear that a higher power has other plans for him."

"Well, as long as he doesn't get half as bad as his grandfather did, he should be okay."

"Don't joke about that!" Pawben exclaimed.

Toadstool held both hands in the air, as if he was under arrest. He looked down at the staff Pawben had set on the floor between them. "Is that the one that the king gave you?"

"The Emperor of Upper Sultry, yes. It came in handy during our ordeal with the Sky Titans."

Toadstool rubbed his hands together and leaned forward. "The next chapter in the epic of Benny Clout! Let's hear it!"

Pawben sat silently for a moment, gently puffing the cigar. He was extremely tired, but didn't want to risk a second episode with a long-deceased loved one. He rolled his eyes and waved his hand over the burning end of the cigar, extinguishing it. He tossed it into the copper spittoon at Toadstool's feet and leaned back.

"Get comfortable, turtle boy. This one is a doozy."

Chapter 1
Benny

Benny woke up on his stomach, face-first in a puddle of what smelled like urine; he was completely naked and his hands were tied behind his back. The foul stench of fecal matter, human and otherwise, greeted his nostrils as he struggled to his knees. He could tell by wiggling his nose that it had been broken and reset, and as he ran his tongue across his upper lip he could taste flakes of dried blood. It was pitch black and, no matter which direction he looked, he could see nothing. He strained to remember where he was and how he'd gotten there, but for the time being his mind was a blank canvas.

"Where the hell am I? Is there anybody there?" he called, greeted only by painful moans and cursing.

"Stop yelling or they'll come back and kill us all," a hoarse voice whispered nearby.

Benny looked in the direction of the voice...as if that would do any good. "Where are we? What's going on?"

"You're in a dungeon, moron, or ain't you noticed?" the same voice whispered again.

He cringed at the feeling of a mud-like substance on his rump as he sat in a more comfortable position. He splayed his legs out in front of him, but quickly pulled them back as he felt a hairy limb brush against his.

"Human?" the voice inquired.

"What'd you expect," Benny responded. "Aren't you human?"

"I'm a Voot...a Tiger man. You're in a Voot dungeon. How hard did they hit you, boy?"

Benny tried his best to remember what had transpired prior to awaking in that hellhole of a dungeon, still to no avail. He knew who the Voot were; a race of Tiger-men, one of which he remembered Helena fighting at the tournament in Upper Sultry. But what was he doing in their compound? "How long have I been here?" he asked the prisoner.

"I've been here for at least a day...maybe two...and they haven't brought anyone in here since before then. You do the math."

"Well, if I got here before you, didn't you see them bring me into your settlement?" Benny asked.

"A few days before they arrested me I saw a patrol of our soldiers come into our city carrying your limp body...but they'd put a hood over your head. They didn't go into particulars as to who you were, and I didn't ask."

"Why are you here?" Benny pried.

"What are you, the question king? Shut up and mind your own business. I told you before that if they catch us talking they'll skin us both."

Benny was annoyed at the Voot's attitude and decided to keep his mouth shut. He sat there for what felt like an eternity before a small door opened at the far end of the room. An armored Voot soldier wearing a plumed helmet and carrying a spear quickly entered, crossing the dungeon cell and grabbing Benny roughly under the armpit.

"What's going on?" Benny asked.

"Shut up and move, human scum!" he barked, practically dragging Benny into a darkly lit hallway.

Benny looked around at his surroundings for the first time. They walked down a narrow stone hallway. Aside from an occasional torch mounted on the wall, and the occasional cell door, it was a void tunnel. Several Voot soldiers passed as Benny was being escorted, and they had no qualms with knocking him out of the way as they did so. Once, Benny fell backwards onto the floor, only to be kicked hard in the gut by his escort. "Get up, you hairless monkey!" he yelled at Benny.

"You know, this would be a hell of a lot easier if you'd just tell me what's going on…"

"You'll find out soon enough, trespasser. Now shut up or the only part of you to meet the elders will be your head on my pike!" The Voot began walking even faster. Benny's feet ached as they pounded the rough stone floor.

Trespassing? Benny thought. It wasn't much of an answer, but at least he knew why he was being imprisoned. He didn't know much about the Voot, aside from that they were a very militaristic race of humanoid tigers and that they lived secluded in various parts of Upper Sultry. Apparently he had somehow wound up on Voot land, uninvited, and got his skull cracked so hard he'd completely lost his memory. Then it hit him; he'd been traveling with Dale Beranger and Helena the Amazon. They were trying to reach some city in the Northern Mountains, but why? Things began coming back in bits and pieces, but not enough for Benny to patch together.

They arrived at a door, which the soldier thrust open, shoving Benny into a dimly lit room. Benny looked around. It seemed to be some sort of bathing room. In the center was a large tub set into the stone floor, and next to it a small wooden table with what looked like folded clothes. On the far wall there was a mirror and a small wooden stool beside it. *All the comforts of home*, Benny thought, rolling his eyes.

"You have thirty minutes to wash yourself and dress. Then you'll go before the city elders to decide your fate. I'll be right outside the door. Try anything and you're dead!" the soldier said before storming back out the door, leaving Benny alone.

He walked over to the tub and saw a small green block of some unknown substance on the floor. Picking it up, he dipped it into the water and rubbed it between his hands to produce lather. Benny sniffed the soap. It smelled like dirty feet, but it was better than feces. He bathed quickly, only to realize after climbing out of the now rank water that there were no towels; he had to drip dry. After shaking himself off like a dog, he dressed in the garments provided. They were of a red silky material, consisting of a pair of loose trousers and a tunic which wrapped around his body at the waist. He slipped them on and walked over to the mirror.

"Lovely," Benny said as he gazed upon his appearance.

His hair, now somewhat clean, was messy and unkempt, and his beard was long and knotted in several spots. The clothing he'd been supplied was wet and clinging to his body, which was especially uncomfortable in the crotch area. He sat down on the stool and leaned against the cold stone wall. For what little time he had, he closed his eyes in rest and attempted to piece together the events that led to this predicament.

+

"It'll take some time for word to spread about his death," said Tele, "and it'll take even more time to harvest the loyal crop from the weeds that will hopefully surrender to Magenta."

"Tele's right. A number of the Kudgels will turn to Magenta, being the same blood of their former leader. But it would be stupid to think they'd all surrender. We still don't know how far this initial rebellion has spread, or what allies Purp had. I have a feeling the forces we've fought so far were just the tip of the iceberg," Dale said, kneeling in the spot where Purp's body had been.

Helena spoke next. "Even so, we can't afford to dawdle. But we can't make for Upper Sultry in our present state. Even an Amazon has her limits."

"I think it's best, all things considered, that we return to Gant, rest, and prepare for the journey," said Virtue. Benny merely sat in silence, the horrors of the night's events just now coming to full realization.

"It looks like you have your hands full." Tele stepped out of the wagon, "I'd love to help further, but my part ends here."

"You've done enough. We owe you one," Dale said, saluting the vampire.

The telepath nodded and quickly fled into the night. Benny was trembling, trying to fight off tears. Dale looked at him, and placed a hand on his shoulder. Benny jerked away violently and crossed to the other end of the wagon. "Can we just get the hell outta here?!" he yelled.

Dale nodded, and assumed his role driving the wagon. They rode in silence back to Gant, and as they arrived at the Fox Den, the first rays of morning were illuminating the sky. Some of the villagers had come out of hiding, and had begun gathering the dead to be buried or burned. When they got to the inn, they saw the blacksmith standing at the door. "I didn't move Jack or any of the bodies in the inn. Figured y'all would want to take care of them yourselves," he said.

Dale walked past him and into the dining hall. Helena walked down to the river, stripped down and began bathing, oblivious to whatever observers there were. *I doubt anyone would care after last night*, Benny thought.

"I'll fill the basin in our room. Go have a drink with Dale and relax for a bit. We have a little time to spare." Virtue kissed his cheek and crossed the bridge to their wing of the inn.

Flack's body was left in the same state as when they'd left. Dale stood over it for a few seconds before reaching down and closing the eyelids. Dale saw Benny and motioned for him to sit down at their table.

"I'll get us a drink…if there's anything left." He left and returned from the wrecked bar with a single bottle of rum. They sat and took turns drinking.

"You're not the only one who's upset," Dale stated.

Benny took a long, hard swig when Dale passed the bottle to him. It burned his throat and tasted like piss, but he kept it down.

"You probably shouldn't get drunk before our big journey," Helena said, entering the room, naked but clean of the blood and grime of battle. She sat down at the table with them.

"The barrels are either destroyed or empty, and this was the only thing I found intact," Dale said. "I normally don't drink alcohol when preparing for a journey, but in this case I'll make an exception. Besides, one bottle between the three of us won't do much." He grabbed the bottle from Benny and handed it to Helena.

"Make that four of us," Virtue said, arriving at the table and taking the bottle from Helena.

"What do we do from here?" Benny asked.

"I guess we'll start by going back up to Bluecorn Betty and use the portal, if it remains unharmed. Hopefully Marty's okay," Dale said.

"He's got a right hook that could knock a dragon loopy. Believe me, he's fine." Helena rubbed her jaw and winked at Dale.

"We'll check on Bum on the way," Virtue said. She briefly explained the events of the Battle at Galver and Elim Dorn, how Bum had been injured, and about Dijon's arrest. Dale winced as he listened to the tale.

"He's tough. He'll be all right, but I doubt he'll be able to join us on our trip. That's a shame. He's a good ranger, and can clip the wings off a fly from a mile away with his crossbow." Dale took a sip after Benny's turn, realized the bottle was now empty, and dropped it on the floor. Benny didn't normally drink, and could already feel the buzz of the alcohol from the few sips he'd taken. The others were obviously more experienced drinkers, since they giggled at him as his eyes began rolling in his head.

"Jack wasn't much of a drinker either. Great swordsman, though. I regret what I did to him." Dale said. The three looked at him, confused. "You know how he had that limp?" Dale asked.

After acknowledging they didn't, Dale explained how he and Jack had once challenged each other to a 'friendly' duel. "After Alsbury, Cycleze, Jack, Marty Danaher, and I joined forces to create a stable of mercenaries. We called ourselves the Ferocious Four."

"You couldn't think of a better name?" Helena laughed.

"We weren't very creative. Anyway, after one of our last jobs together, Jack and I got drunk and started arguing over who the better fighter was. Jack's dad had just bought this place, and we were visiting. We fought right out in the street, there. We started off with our swords, and fought for what seemed like hours. We weren't really trying to hurt each other at first, but we were both drunk and after we nicked each other it got more serious. Jack was thin and agile, and I was at my strongest and meanest. It got ugly."

"Jack, thin?" Benny asked. Benny had always known Jack as the fat, bald, mustached man he had been at death.

"He didn't always have that gut, or that bald dome either. Anyhow, we broke our swords after some particularly hard blows and it spilled into a wrestling match. I thought I'd beat Jack easily once that happened, but he danced circles around me." Dale laughed. "I looked like a blundering idiot out there. He put moves on me I've never seen since. I got embarrassed, and then angry. The rest is history."

"What did you do?" Helena asked.

"We may have been drunk, but we'd agreed to fight fair: no low blows, eye gouging, or any cheap shots like that. I wanted to out-skill Jack, but when I realized he had me beat, I broke our rules and threw sand in his eyes. If it'd been a real fight, I know Jack would've been ready for it, but like I said, we'd set rules. It stunned him and I tackled him at the knees. I heard the bone snap, but I continued beating on him once I got him to the ground. Took ten men to get me off. He recovered, and we made amends, but his leg was shot. He was never the same man after that." Dale buried his face in his hands.

"Why'd you tell us that?" Benny was confused. He knew how Dale had once been and wasn't angry nor surprised by the story, but what had spawned Dale's sudden confession?

"If we're going to be traveling together, I don't want any secrets between us. I was a very bad person. Alsbury wasn't my only ill deed. I was a bully...I didn't care about anyone, not even my closest friends, Marty and Jack. I didn't have the best childhood, and I let those who'd hurt me in the past turn me into a monster. For a long time I used the excuse that it was Cycleze's brainwashing that did it to me, but he was only feeding the virus that was already inside me." He looked Benny in the eyes. "And when you snapped at me in the wagon, I could see myself in you. I know you're upset about Jack and Nap, but don't let it affect who you are. You're a good person. I want you to stay that way."

"I guess you're going to tell us you're the one responsible for Marty Danaher getting his earlobes ripped off, too?" Benny joked.

"To be quite frank, yes, I was. He got drunk before we were supposed to do a job, and I got angry. I took him to a goblin camp late one night and stapled his earlobes to a tree," Dale said. The others were silent.

"Well, it doesn't matter now. Jack's dead, Marty's probably dead, and we have a long trip ahead of us. The sooner we get this over with, the better." Benny stood up, wobbly, and Virtue helped him back to their room.

"The boy's in a delicate state right now...don't put too much on him," Helena said, walking over to Dale and holding his head against her chest. "We need rest. Come to bed and let me take things off your mind."

Dale grew annoyed and stood up. "How can you think of knocking boots at a time like this?"

"You're being an ass. I'm trying to comfort you, not get in your pants. We may not be officially married yet, but I'm your wife, and it's my duty to be there for you."

Dale walked back to Helena and held her close. "I'm sorry. I just need to be alone right now. I'm going to go spend some time with Jack before I decide what to do with his body, and the others. Get some rest. We're heading out tomorrow at dusk."

Helena said nothing, but Dale knew she understood. She kissed him passionately before leaving him alone in the dining hall.

When Benny woke up, the sun was setting in the west. Dale had buried Flack and burned the other Kudgel bodies. Benny was depressed they couldn't give all the bodies a proper burial, but there simply wasn't time or space in Gant to do so. Flack's burial was already finished, a shallow grave under a tree by the river. A stick was placed to mark it until a more permanent headstone could be made. Benny noticed Dale had hung Flack's rat-faced hood on the stick marking his grave.

Benny noticed Dale kneeling next to the grave, silently praying. When he saw Benny, he stood up. "I went ahead and buried Flack. I wanted to wait to fill in Jack's grave until you could say goodbye."

"Thank you," Benny said.

Jack looked peaceful. Dale had put clean clothes on him, as well as the dirty cook's apron Jack had been so fond of wearing. His sword, the one with the teeth, which Jack had let Benny borrow during his initial journey with Dale and Cycleze, lay on his chest. As Benny grabbed a shovel, Dale handed him something. "Here. Jack would want you to have this. I found it under his bed." It was a small, green felt cap with a long, red feather sticking out of it. It looked rather comical, and Benny looked at Dale in confusion.

"This was Jack's trademark. Back in the day he'd never be caught dead without it." Dale said.

Benny smiled at Dale and put the cap on his head. For a split second, Dale began to tear up, but preoccupied himself with filling in the grave. When finished, they returned to find Helena and Virtue loading supplies into the wagon.

"We all set?" Virtue asked.

"Yes, except for one thing," Dale said, "I don't want you going with us, Virtue." Benny looked at Dale, confused, but Dale was quick to continue. "You are with child, and there's no telling how long this journey will be. Someone also needs to stay and watch over the Fox Den. When Dale and I visit Bum, we'll ask him if he can come protect you."

"I guess you have a point," Virtue walked over to Benny and held his hand.

"It'll be harder without you...both emotionally and practically. But I think Dale has a point. I don't want anything happening to you, or our child. I don't know if I can go that long without you, though..." Benny leaned against Virtue.

"What about your telepathy?" Helena chimed in. "Can it work long distance?"

"I'm not sure. It might take time and practice for me to reach out that far, and it may get harder the further north y'all travel, but maybe it'll work."

"Then perhaps we won't be separated entirely," Benny said.

"Oh, Benny, you almost forgot," Virtue ran back into the Fox Den and returned with the staff he'd won at the tournament. "You should learn to use this on your travels. It could come in handy."

Benny thanked Virtue, kissing her passionately. Then, silently, they boarded the wagon and departed.

✦

It took only about a day and a half to reach Galver Dorn, and the new Duke met them as they rode in. He greeted everyone, revealing his name to be Ames Murdock. "It seems in the haste of battle I never got a chance to introduce myself," he said to Benny.

"Benny Clout, and this is my friend, Dale Beranger, and his wife, Helena." Benny shook Murdock's hand, "How's Bum?"

"Beranger? Oh yes, you were Dijon's errand boy. The orc is doing well. He's actually helping with repairs in the city square."

"Errand boy?" Helena asked Dale as they headed for the city square.

"Eh...don't ask," Dale chuckled.

They found Bum, with his head bandaged and his arm in a sling, slowly aiding the townsfolk in piling up debris and bodies. He saw the trio and rushed, or rather hobbled, over to greet them. He and Dale embraced. "Don't let these bandages fool you. In a few more days they said I should be right as rain, short of a few handsome scars."

They quickly filled him in on the events that had transpired since Benny, Virtue, and Liverwart parted ways with the orc. He understood, and was quick to accept the duty of watching over Virtue. "I'll be glad to help out at the inn, as soon as I finish helping these men here. It appears as if there was a second wave of Kudgels that attacked Elim Dorn after we left, and we need to accommodate the refugees."

"Will they try for Galver Dorn?" Helena asked.

"It doesn't appear so. They sent a messenger to discuss terms of peace. They are low on supplies and fever is spreading through their troops. We told them, as long as they stay in Elim Dorn, we'll leave them alone, and they agreed to leave us be as well."

"We'd love to stick around and make sure they live up to their word, but we need to be going," Dale said. They exchanged farewells and parted ways.

It took them several days to reach Bluecorn Betty, only stopping to exchange places in the driver's seat. When they reached the castle, things didn't look good. Bodies littered the ground outside the main structure, and parts of the castle were still smoldering from fire. But it was when they saw the water spirit's pool underneath the castle that Dale got worried. Dale had saved the spirit once before when her original home pond dried up, and the spirit had thanked him by considering Dale her adoptive son. Benny doubted Dale could save her now though. Dead Kudgels were littered around and in the water; the womanly figure of the water spirit was only half formed from the waist up. She was lying face down on the bank like a beached whale. Dale ran to her and carefully rolled her over.

"Mom?" he called to her. She slowly reached up a hand, which melted back into water as it touched his face, splashing down on Dale's pants.

"What's wrong with her?" Benny asked.

Dale was frantic. "Her pool is her life-force. If it's contaminated she'll die." He cupped some water in his hand and spat it back out, "The Kudgels poisoned it!"

"Can we do anything?" Helena asked.

Dale looked up and around frantically. "I don't know…she's one of the last of her kind, and I know very little about her. Benny, get me a bottle!"

Benny ran to the wagon, found a small flask, and ran back to Dale. Almost all but the spirit's head and chest had dissipated back into water. She looked up at Dale. She was sad, but at the same time, she looked relieved to know he was okay, and that he was with her. Dale held the flask down to her. She nodded and dissipated back into water, entering the flask.

"The wizard might know how to purify her. Then maybe I can find new water for her to live in. This is an enchanted flask to keep liquids fresh. Marty gave it to Jack a long time ago...I found it with that hat I gave you, Benny. It was used for Marty's whiskey...it might help Mom."

"Speaking of the old slugger, let's go see if he's all right," Helena suggested.

They climbed up to the floor with the inn and tavern, and found the front door broken off its hinges. No sound came from inside, but a dead Kudgel, his face bashed in, lay on the threshold. For the first time since he'd known him, Benny saw true fear in Dale's eyes.

"What is it?" Helena asked.

Dale looked at Helena and Benny. "I thought he'd quit drinking...he told me he had. This isn't good."

"What the hell are you talking about?" Benny asked.

"Marty...he used to get drunk before fights and jobs...he's a tough fighter, but when he got drunk he became a demon. That was why I gave him over to the goblin camp. He'd become so ferocious when he drank, he'd go on killing sprees, even after a job was done. Nobody can stop him when he's like this, not even me. The only thing you can do is keep him drinking until he passes out."

"As rough and tumble as he was with us Amazons, sober, I'd hate to fight him like that." Helena grabbed her sword.

"No, put your sword away. He'll kill you before you can make the first strike."

"He's that quick?" Benny asked.

"He's quicker." Dale said.

"Now I see why he joined forces with you and Cycleze," Benny said.

Helena shook her head. "After this is all over, you're gonna have to tell me who this Cycleze fellow is. Hell, let's get this over with."

They stepped over the body of the Kudgel and entered a pitch black dining hall. Tables and chairs were thrown everywhere, and bodies of Kudgels and patrons were everywhere, most of them with their faces smashed. Dale entered first, with Helena and Benny behind him. Benny held his staff in front of him. Not knowing how to operate it, he doubted it'd do much good. Then, a deep, menacing voice issued from the darkness. It was the voice of Marty Danaher, but there was definitely something different about it. It was slurred and irrational.

"More pigs to the slaughter," Marty laughed maniacally. "Have you so easily forgotten what I am? I am the madness within you…begging to be released from the furthest depths of your pathetic little animal mind. I am what you cower from in your bed at night…waiting to taste your blood and drink your soul!"

"Marty, cut the crap! It's me, Dale."

"Marty is dead, just like you're about to be!" A body rushed out from the darkness.

Marty slammed into Dale, gripping him in a bear hug and slamming him into the wall, splintering wood and taking Dale to the floor. He slammed his fist into Dale's face. Dale managed to reverse positions, blood pouring from his nostrils. He did his best to grab onto Marty's arms, but Marty screamed like an animal and threw Dale off him like a rag doll. Helena rushed in to meet him, sword drawn, but Marty stuck out his leg and kicked her hard in the groin and then the face. Marty came after Benny, but Dale grabbed the man from behind and tried to hold him in place. "Marty, knock it off, it's Dale! It's Dale Beranger!"

The moonlight shone in through the doorway and illuminated Marty's face: his eyes were blood red and saliva dripped from his mouth. His knuckles were raw and bloodstained, and his left pinkie was broken backwards. After Dale screamed his name several more times, a sadistic grin came across Marty's face. "Beranger?" he asked.

"Yes! It's me! It's Dale!" Dale held on for dear life, shaking with the strain of trying to hold the tall, scrawny man in place.

"You want them? We'll split their skulls and eat their brains…"

"No! They're friends. Drinking buddies!"

At that, Marty broke loose from Dale and looked at him strangely. "Drink?" he asked.

"Yes. Come on, Marty. Let's drink, just like the good ol' days."

Marty slapped Dale and began laughing, stumbling as he walked towards a booth. He slumped into a chair and began breathing heavily. In the shadows, he looked like a demon from the darkest pits of hell. His face was frail and emaciated, and his nose started to bleed. "Benny, grab all the liquor you can find! Now!" Dale screamed.

Benny ran behind what remained of the bar and found several bottles of a dark liquid he couldn't place, and brought them back to Dale. He handed one to Marty, who broke off the neck and chugged the substance. He downed the other bottles Benny brought, smashing each into the table when finished. "More?" he asked.

"Yes! We got loads more! Benny?" Dale's voice was filled with worry.

"Yeah...hold..." Benny nearly tripped over a dead Kudgel trying to get back to the bar. He tried one of the beer barrels, and it still had some in it. He grabbed a few metal pints off the ground and filled them to the brim. When he brought them back to Marty, the man shoved him back and chugged them both in a matter of moments. They repeated this process, bringing whatever liquid they could to Marty's lips. After what seemed like an eternity, and an ungodly amount of alcohol, Marty began to burp loudly. He sat still for a few minutes, hiccupping, and then vomited all over himself and the table. He collapsed out of his chair, and then spewed more vomit. The stream of ale and liquor seemed to go on without end from his mouth, and finally, after incoherent garble, Marty collapsed in his own juices. He was at last unconscious.

"Quickly, roll him over on his side before he chokes." Benny and Dale rolled Marty onto his side.

Helena stirred. "What the bloody hell!?" she screamed.

Marty began to moan, and Dale sat down beside him. "He's fine now. He'll have a hell of a hangover, but he's okay."

They sat in silence for a while before Marty began to stir, looking up at Helena with a dazed look of ecstasy. "I'm pooping," Marty muttered, grinning like an idiot. A bubbling sound issued from his rump, and a putrid smell followed. Benny nearly choked and walked to the other side of the room, followed by Helena. Dale stayed by Marty's side, pinching his nose.

"It's okay, buddy," he said, "We'll worry about it in the morning."

Helena, despite being knocked out briefly by Marty earlier, offered to watch him for the night to make sure he didn't choke on his own vomit. As the morning hours drew close, the effects of the alcohol wore off and Marty slowly aroused. He was obviously hung over, talking slowly and not moving much except to clean up and change clothing.

"When did you guys get here?" Marty said, picking up a chair to sit down in the dining hall.

"Shortly before you gave birth to the brown monster," Helena said, motioning to the stain on the floor where Marty had soiled himself. Marty looked ashamed.

"I haven't drank like that in years. We received word from a scout that the Kudgels were coming this way, and I got upset and began drinking. I don't remember anything since." He looked down at a dead Kudgel. "Did I do all this?"

"Let's just say we had a little sparring session of our own when we arrived. You ranted about strange stuff and then attacked us. I managed to convince you of who I was, so we filled you up till you burst your bubble," Dale said.

Marty shrugged. "About the only thing you could do, I reckon."

Benny stared at the now sober Marty. To look at him, Benny didn't see how he could have been capable of killing so many with his bare hands. He was tall and scrawny, and aside from the short shock of brown hair and missing earlobes, had no distinguishing features. Then Benny remembered as a teenager how alcohol made his older brother Aiken belligerent and uncontrollable, and understood.

"Do you know if there are any survivors?" Benny asked.

"Huh? Oh, I don't know. Probably not. Most left after we heard the Kudgels were coming, and only myself and a few others stayed to try and protect the castle."

"What about the bell tower?" Dale asked. "Did the wizard and his dwarf pull through?"

"Dunno...you'll have to check it out for yourselves."

"Well, we'll leave you to take care of this. We have bigger fish to fry," Helena said.

"I guess this initial attack isn't the last of their tricks?" Marty asked.

"Not if we don't stop them." Then Dale quickly filled Marty in.

Marty nodded. "Well, you'll want to get going I guess. I'll be okay. Thanks for looking after me. Sorry Benny and the lass had to see my ugly side. I'd like to repay you somehow."

"We'll take a rain check." Dale laughed and shook Marty's hand before leaving with Helena and Benny.

They arrived at Siegfried's Bell Tower to see the wizard's assistant, the randy, purple-haired dwarf, stacking dead bodies. His right hand was wrapped and stained through with blood. He smiled upon seeing Helena, but frowned when he realized Benny and Dale were right behind.

"You won't get very far. That old coot fled through the portal, blowing it to pieces behind him. Left me to fend for myself."

"Damn!" Dale yelled.

"At least you still have all your digits, scarface." He held up his bandaged hand. "Got my thumb bit off."

"How'd you manage to survive?" Helena asked.

The dwarf puffed up his chest and picked up a hefty battle ax that was lying by his feet. "Pleasing women ain't the only thing I'm good at," he winked at Helena and ran his tongue across his lips. Helena rolled her eyes.

"Cool it, lover boy," Dale said.

"Oh, come on. I was nearly killed. Humor me at least!" He dropped his ax and began dragging a dead Kudgel towards the building pile.

"Is there anything you can do about that portal?" Dale asked.

The dwarf laughed. "Not in this lifetime, butt face."

"We have to get to the Northern Mountains…to the city of the frost dwarves. That portal was going to save us valuable time."

"Frost dwarves? You mean Alfen Gulfadex?"

"What's that?" Benny asked.

"That's what they call it…Alfen Gulfadex…holy city of the frost dwarves. I got some cousins who live there," the dwarf said.

Dale frowned and crossed his arms. "Well, since the portal is null and void, what's the best way to get there?"

The dwarf pointed to Dale's feet and started laughing.

"Great!" Dale complained.

They turned and began walking back down the tower. The dwarf ran after them. "Wow, hold on a sec. You're just going to leave me here?"

"I'd say join us, but I doubt you'd be much help…aside from trying to get between my legs," Helena said.

The dwarf held his ax in front of him. "I know how to fight. And I can help you get to Alfen Gulfadex."

Dale shrugged. "Come on, then. What's your name, horny toad?"

"Burgundy," the dwarf said. "Just call me Burgundy."

+

Virtue was lonely without Benny. It had only been a day since they'd departed, but it seemed like a lifetime. Virtue lay curled up in bed, wrapped in blankets to stave off the cold mountain air. She didn't notice the smoke that breathed in from under the door and windows. Black as night, it crawled across the floor to the far corner of the room. Slowly it began to take form, feet first, until a dark figure stood concealed in the shadows.

"Laurel," he called.

Virtue recognized the voice even from sleep, and the name which had once been hers. Memories of the past came flooding back. The voice was distant and hollow: a dark, brooding accent that had once made her feel so loved and protected.

"It can't be," she gasped.

"So quick to doubt, my love?" he said.

"I thought you were..."

"Dead?" he cut her off. His voice remained calm, but Virtue could hear the menace growing within it.

"Why didn't you come sooner? I didn't know you survived."

"How could you not know? You were there when it happened! You could've checked my body...you could have known!"

"I was scared...the vampires tore you apart. I was injured."

"Excuses are like armpits, dear. Everybody has one." She saw a gloved hand rise into the shaft of moonlight emanating from the window, pointing at Benny's clothes draped across the chair beside her. "And yes, I do know about *him*."

Virtue grew terrified. "What are you going to do? Please, don't hurt him. He doesn't know."

"So you lied about your past? How quaint!"

"You don't understand! I beg of you, please…"

His laugh was loud and callous. "Don't you worry, love. I won't harm a hair on his head. I'm under direct orders not to…and besides, it's not his fault you fell in love with him."

"I never stopped loving you…but he is my husband now. I love him, too. Don't you understand? I thought you were dead. Did you want me to suffer through life alone?" Virtue's voice was shaky, and tears streamed down her eyes.

"You'll get yours soon enough, dear Laurel. It's just a shame that poor Benny had to get involved."

"Wait, how did you know his name?!"

He laughed again, and the wickedness that filled it scared Virtue unlike anything she'd ever experienced in her entire life. "We have good plans for ol' Benny boy…and for you."

With that, he dissipated into smoke, and flew like a torrent into Virtue's face. She gasped for air, the life squeezed out of her like a vice. Laughter filled her ears and soon she was unconscious.

Chapter 2
Helena

One moment she had fought for her life, fleeing from Kudgel ghouls and the shadow of their wyrm circling overhead. Then, after a split second blackout, she was coming to her senses, buried underneath a pile of animal furs. She erupted from sleep, sitting in her bed, fists raised and ready for battle. She absorbed her surroundings as her eyes adjusted. Dim candlelight glowed beside her bed, and Helena looked over to see the grinning face of a young, fair-haired girl. It was nighttime, judging by the window above the foot of Helena's bed, but she could see a garland of wildflowers hanging on the child's brow, with the moonlight illuminating the gap-toothed grin as the child sat silently. Finally, after staring Helena down, the little girl spoke. "You could thank me, you know."

"Huh?"

"It's common courtesy to thank people when they save your life."

"I was chased by Kudgels..." Helena sat up, dizzily, "and then a dragon. How did you scare them off?"

The girl shrugged nonchalantly. "Scare them off? Well, my illusion did." She stood up and lit a few more candles on the dresser with the one she held in her hand. "What were you doing in the woods by yourself, anyway? And unarmed nonetheless! I thought grown-ups knew better."

Helena strained to remember what had happened. She knew that Dale, Benny, and herself had been making the long trek by foot into Upper Sultry when they were ambushed and tortured by Kudgel soldiers, and she remembered fleeing through the wilderness, the Kudgels and their dragon hot on her trail. But then there was a blank spot on the canvas. "I was traveling with some friends and I think we got separated."

"They dead?"

Helena was a little taken aback by the casual way the girl asked the question. "I hope not." She noticed her wrist was bandaged. "Where am I?"

"Daddy and I were hunting…well, Daddy was hunting… and I snuck along, following him. He was gonna fight off those creatures, but I spun an illusion that an army of giants were charging behind us, and they scattered. Daddy was upset that I'd tagged along." She laughed at her last remark.

"Daddy?"

"My pa…he's sleeping now. You've been out cold all afternoon since we found you. He didn't want to bring you home, but I made him. He thinks I'm in bed too, but I wanted to stay here till you awoke. I wanted to look at your scars and tattoos. I like them, but Daddy thinks they make you look trashy." She danced around, her attention span obviously waning.

Helena touched her head. There was a kind of bandage there. Oh—that was the result of her torture. "Did you put this on?" she asked.

"Yes. You must have caught your hair something awful. I put some magic salve on so your hair would regrow, and the bandage. It'll be okay in a few days if you leave it alone."

"Thank you," Helena said sincerely.

"Sure."

"I need to speak to your father."

"Later." The girl walked towards the door. "He gets upset when you wake him. He'll probably be out fetching squirrel for breakfast when you wake up, but you'll talk to him, don't worry. But don't be shocked if he doesn't take too kindly to you."

The girl disappeared through the black doorway. "Wait, I don't even know your name!"

The girl poked her head back through the door, with the same grin stretching from ear to ear. "I'm Noletta," she said.

"And your father? I'd like to at least know who I'm bunking with."

"Nolan," she said. "Nolan Ducat."

Helena was shocked when she heard the name. Ever since she was a child, the myths and legends of Nolan Ducat, the Dragon Slayer, had ruminated throughout Lower Sultry; tales of an adventurer who'd killed a dragon with his bare hands. Helena had always been inspired by the tales in her youth, and often impersonated Nolan's character when hunting for her tribe. Helena knew that most people, even today, throughout Upper and Lower Sultry, claimed Nolan was long since dead, the exact details varying between accounts. Once an adult, Helena had passed the stories off as simple fables...fabrications made to entertain little children. There was no way the girl could be telling the truth.

"Nolan Ducat? You mean *the* Nolan Ducat? *The* Dragon Slayer?" Helena was skeptical.

Noletta giggled. "He don't like people knowing his name...but I like seeing the reactions on people's faces when I tell them. He'll probably tan my hide for it, but when your daddy's famous, you gotta milk it for all it's worth!"

Helena was once again left in silence, wondering if the man she'd meet tomorrow really was her childhood hero.

Helena was awoken the next morning by the distant call of dragon fire. It was a deep, bellowing noise that shook the walls and lifted the floorboards. Jumping naked from the bed, she panicked when she couldn't find her weapons. Leaving the room, she found herself on the upstairs balcony of the log cabin, looking down into the living area where Noletta sat by the hearth, calmly eating a muffin.

"Don't just sit there, you stupid child! Bring me my sword, find a crossbow! Didn't you hear the dragon?" Helena, ignoring the stairs, leaped over the wooden handrail and fell some ten feet onto the floor below her. Noletta, instead of jumping into action, clapped at the display of acrobatic skill.

"That was amazing! What else can you do?" She dropped the muffin and mocked Helena's jump with her own over a chair.

Helena ignored the oblivious child and looked around for her swords. Finally, she spotted them sticking out of a barrel at the other end of the room. Not even stopping for the door, she snatched them and slammed through the crude wooden door of the home. She found herself standing on a roofed porch in the chilly air of the forested foothills. The home seemed to be at the crest of the hill, and at the foot Helena spotted the coming danger. Several dozen Kudgels were charging up the rise, screaming and waving their swords in the air. And above them, in the air, Helena spotted the form of a great red dragon, with a Kudgel rider mounted on its back. If it were only the soldiers she wouldn't be worried, but it would take an entire party of warriors to even think of fighting a dragon.

Nonetheless, she would kill them all or die trying. Just as she raised her sword to charge towards the Kudgels, a mighty hand grabbed her and threw her back with a strength that surprised her. "Fight smart, not hard," a gruff voice said.

Helena looked up to see a man dressed in animal skins, a hood concealing his head and face. He was large by human standards, but not enormous, and it looked at first as if his left arm was wrapped within his cloak. He was walking to a large crossbow mounted to a pillar supporting the porch. Helena had failed to notice it at first, and noticed that, unlike most crossbows, it had a crank and pinion on the side to draw back the string and set the arrow. With his right hand he quickly cranked back the string and set a slender arrow with a red ball on the end into the flight groove.

"You're slow as molasses! It's going to take more than one arrow to stop them," Helena snapped.

Then the man released the arrow, which went flying into the crowd of incoming Kudgels. Suddenly, an explosion rocked the hillside, and Kudgel body parts spewed into the air like the burst of fireworks.

The man pulled back his hood to reveal long gray hair and a beard, a single strip of brown streaking down from under his lip, "Noletta? Get your ass out here and bring another red hot!"

The girl came skipping out onto the porch nonchalantly, handing another of the explosive arrows to the man. Clinching the rod in his teeth, he cranked back the string again, set the bolt, and with tremendous strength ripped the entire crossbow from the mount.

Helena was impressed by the man's take-charge attitude, but doubted the crossbow, as large as it was, would effectively reach a moving target like the dragon. Out of the corner of her eye she noticed Noletta, giggling.

"Daddy knows what he's doing," she said.

"That's Nolan?" In the rush of adrenaline brought on by the attack, Helena hadn't stopped to guess at who the old man was, but now she guessed it had been obvious. The dragon circled closer and closer. Though it was doubtful Nolan's crossbow could reach that sort of distance, neither Nolan nor his child seemed worried, and Helena decided to let Nolan take care of things. Time to see if this man really was the dragon slayer of legend.

"Might as well pack it in and go home. It'll never reach!" Helena teased Nolan, testing his mettle.

"That's why I'm letting 'em get closer, you bitchy old screech owl!" Nolan raised the crossbow into the air and aimed into the sky. "They need to be real close."

The dragon, upon seeing Nolan, took a nosedive, spinning through the air as he flew straight at the man. The wyrm flew closer and closer, until it was only a couple hundred feet away. Helena set down her weapon, crossed her arms and waited for events to unfold.

The dragon was getting close, less than a hundred feet, and Helena could see its mouth opening, the glow of fire deep in its throat. Just when it was about to roast Nolan, the old man released the arrow, which Helena saw fly straight into its mouth. There was a marvelous explosion, and what was once the dragon's head and neck came raining down on Nolan in what was almost a mist. Larger, cindering chunks fell afterwards, and the rest of the dragon's body fell in a quivering lump only a few feet from Nolan. The Kudgel rider, covered in war paint, erupted from the charred body in a fury, and came at the unsuspecting Nolan, who was picking up a chunk of the dragon's meat.

With the man not responding to her warning, Helena instinctively launched her broadsword at the Kudgel.

Nolan Ducat dropped the chunk of meat he was inspecting and caught the sword by the handle as it spun through the air at its target. *You're the one not paying attention, dummy,* Helena thought as Nolan gave an annoyed look at the warrior-woman. He back-kicked the Kudgel and sliced a large but superficial gash across the rider's painted chest. The war symbols became skewed with blood as the Kudgel staggered back, with Nolan driving him farther back with a tremendous heel stomp to the man's chest which nearly flipped him backwards. He cut another non-lethal wound into the man's thigh before dropping the sword and bending down to whisper something into his ear. The dragon rider's face contorted in fear as he shook his head up and down, as if agreeing to some terms unknown to Helena. The Kudgel scurried off back down the hill, and Nolan casually picked up a chunk of charred dragon meat. Looking back at Helena, he laughed.

"Why'd you let him go?" Helena asked.

"After the words of advice I just gave him, I doubt those Kudgels will ever set foot on this hill again. Even if they did, it's no big deal. I have far better ways of dispatching foes. What you saw here was just the tip of the iceberg."

"That fiend was going to fry us all to a crisp." Helena placed her hands on her hips, not concerned with the way Nolan looked at her naked form.

"There are two reasons I let him keep his hide. One: so he can relay my message to the rest of his company, if there is any. And two: any man who can tame and ride a red dragon can't be all bad." He winked at Helena and gave a quick look at her pierced nipple, "You better just be thankful I can't get a hard on anymore, little lady. If I was a few years younger, you'd be in some trouble." Nolan whistled a cat call and carried the chunk of meat into the house.

"And I suppose that's dinner?" Helena pointed to the dragon meat.

"Unless you'd rather starve," Nolan gave his daughter a stern look, "Remount my crossbow."

"Do I have to? I wanna talk to her." She pointed to Helena.

"You don't have to do anything, just like I don't have to give you dinner either." Nolan walked back into the house.

Helena chuckled. *I guess it's Nolan after all,* she thought

Before Helena could realize, Noletta had somehow picked up the massive crossbow and remounted it to the porch. It'd been less than five seconds.

"Don't mind Daddy. He don't like company, that's all."

"I figured he was just playing hard-to-get."

Noletta shrugged and walked to the doorway.

Helena was given some of Nolan's clothing—smelly, thick, and oversized—and she sat at the dinner table before the hearth while Nolan cut up chunks of the dragon meat. "I didn't know you could eat dragon," Helena said.

"Aren't many left…most people think they're extinct, so naturally people forgot what a delicacy it is. It's hard to get to the meat…but those exploding arrows I crafted are powerful enough to penetrate their scales."

"You crafted those arrows?" Nolan paused the carving and grabbed another one of the red-tipped arrows to show Helena. She took a closer look at the tip. "Runes?" she asked.

"Learned them from an old elf magician. The ball is basically hardened clay made from various materials that only explode on impact when the rune is activated. If it weren't for the runes, they'd explode at the slightest touch."

"How do you activate the runes?" Helena asked.

"An incantation." He set the arrow on the table.

"What's the incantation?"

"Ain't gonna tell ya." Nolan continued with his previous duties. "But you *could* tell me, girl, what you're doing on my property and who those ruffians are out there."

Helena tried to explain, but found the details of her memory to be somewhat hazy. Nolan obviously grew irritated by her silence.

"I went through the trouble of fighting those bastards off, twice, and killed a damn dragon to save your hide. My privacy is precious to me and, after years of peace and solitude, it's ruined by some bitch in the buff." He glared at her, holding out his hand, "And I'd like my weapons back, please."

"Weapons?" Helena asked, looking at her swords which she'd laid in her lap. She realized quickly that Noletta had told her the night before she was unarmed when she was found. The swords were obviously not hers; they were too finely crafted to be hers. These swords belonged in a museum, not some shack out in the wilderness. Nonetheless, they belonged to Nolan.

"I'm sorry," she placed them on the table, "I panicked when I heard the dragon and grabbed the first swords I saw."

Nolan grabbed the sheathed swords with one hand and put them back where Helena had found them. He then took off his thick buckskin jacket and hung it on the pommels of those swords. As he came back into the light, Helena was amazed. She had assumed earlier that Nolan had wrapped his arm inside his jacket due to some injury, but where she expected to see an arm in a sling, there was a mottled lump of flesh just after the shoulder. He wore a smudged, sleeveless white tunic which fit tightly to his torso; it was obvious his left arm was removed quite some time ago.

"Something wrong?" He held up his muscular right arm, patting himself and looking down sardonically.

"No, I just didn't realize…"

"…realize what? That I was missing an arm?" He set a plate of charred red meat in front of Helena and then gave Noletta a smaller portion.

"It's not a big deal…I've seen warriors with more severe injuries." It was a true statement. "I'm more surprised that you're alive at all, to be honest. I was beginning to think the legendary Nolan Ducat didn't even exist." She chuckled.

He walked over to what Helena assumed was a pantry. "Legendary?"

"Yes, Mr. Ducat. There aren't many who haven't heard of your exploits."

"Well, listen here, whoever-you-are…most of what you've heard about me is either highly exaggerated or completely false."

He walked over to a barrel of beer and began to fill the cups. He stopped at the last, apparently realizing there was still something in it, and took a sip. "Oh, that beer is definitely rotten!" he said, coughing and spitting as he poured the cup's contents on the floor. He then filled it with beer and looked back at Helena. "That cup will be mine."

"You still didn't answer my question," Nolan stated. "What were you doing on my property?"

"Good luck on that, Daddy. I asked her already and she don't remember a thing." Noletta was already digging into her dragon meat with her bare hands.

"If you expect to receive my hospitality, I strongly suggest you *start* remembering." Nolan's voice dripped with menace.

"I honestly don't remember exactly...I know I was traveling north with some companions, Benny Clout, Dale Beranger, and ..." At that moment Nolan held a hand up at Helena. The look on his face made Helena's hair stand on end. It was the first time Helena had ever been scared of another human, let alone a man.

"Dale who?" His face trembled with anger.

"Dale Beranger, he was one of my compa—" Helena was cut short.

Nolan had leaped from his seat across the table, tackling Helena to the floor with his right hand on her neck, choking the life from her. Normally, she would have used her grappling skills to escape, or perhaps reverse Nolan's choke into an arm bar or a similar hold, but Nolan's grip was far too strong, and Helena was too gripped with fear to attempt anything. All she heard before she began to black out was Nolan's warning, "Speak my son's name again and I'll gut you like a pig!"

Dawn was approaching by the time Virtue and Bum had cleaned the last of the mess made by the patrons of the tavern. The miners (who were mostly dwarves) on the other side of the Gant Mountains had struck the mother lode of precious metal and gems, and to celebrate, they bought drinks for everyone in Gant. It meant a heavy payday, or night, for the Fox Den, but it also meant there'd be no rest until the sun appeared in the east.

"Thanks, Bum." Virtue slung a soiled cleaning rag over her shoulder. "I haven't seen a night like that since Jack passed."

Bum rearranged some chairs that had been knocked over escorting a particularly drunk dwarf from the establishment. "I'm glad it's over, to be honest. I had to break up three brawls tonight. I don't think I'm made for the bouncer's life. Lucky that giant got here a few hours ago to clear the place out...it wouldn't be bad if Dale or Benny were still here to help."

Virtue paused, and tears began to well up in her eyes. It had only been a matter of weeks, but it felt like a century. She had spent every day right by Benny's side for almost 6 years, and now it seemed as if Benny had never even existed. Failed attempts at long distance telepathy hadn't achieved fruition, and without an experienced mentor (the vampire, Tele, couldn't be located and had likely fled the region), she was left by herself to spend most of her spare time studying. She began to sob and Bum held her.

"I'm sorry, bat girl. Benny's going to be okay...they all will. Keep practicing with that mind-talking thing you were telling me about. With your talent, it'll pull through in no time."

As they hugged, they failed to notice the eerie black smoke crawling through the floor boards around their feet. With her vision blurred by tears and buried in Bums chest, she didn't even notice the dark-haired man form from the vapors less than a foot behind Bum.

"There anyone in this town you haven't fornicated with?" By the time Virtue recognized the voice from her past, the figure had bit Bum in the neck. He flew like a bat out of hell over the orc's falling body, pinning Virtue to the floor. "And with an orc, of all types? I never took you for a bottom feeder, Laurel."

Virtue gasped for breath as the man pressed his body into hers, grinding his man parts hard into her private region. He ripped her leggings off like tissue paper and, after revealing his own fifth appendage, proceeded to rape his former lover. Virtue fought to get away from him, but she couldn't.

"Ammarod...please!" She thought speaking his name would trigger some act of mercy, reach whatever remote goodness was left inside the one she had once loved and, in fact, still loved. The man violently drilled himself into her repeatedly, his face hovering as sweat dripped off his nose into her eyes. Ammarod, whose embrace had once been so tender and compassionate, was a wild animal, and Virtue was beginning to bleed. Out of desperation, she dug her long fingernails into his wrist, which stunned Ammarod just enough for her to get out of his choke hold. "HELP!" she cried.

"You bitch!" Ammarod brought the full force of his forearm into her face as she continued to scream. Finally silencing her, he rose to his feet, redressed, and drew a rapier from his unfastened sword belt.

"Help..." Virtue gasped through bloodied lips, crawling away from the figure who was about to kill her.

"Help won't come, Laurel. You'll be left to die, alone, unloved...just like I was!"

Just then, a massive figure broke through the door frame, taking the doors off the hinges and knocking over tables. Liverwart stood at his full eight feet, panting hard but ready for a fight. He'd been carrying an intoxicated townsman home when he'd heard Virtue's scream. Now he was in a rage, and eager to find the source of her trouble.

"You hurt friend! Me hurt you!" Liverwart screamed.

Ammarod laughed. "I am like smoke, mist, and vapor. I move like a cool breeze on a warm summer day. I can strike like lightning in a thunderstorm, and come over you like a cyclone. You are slow, fat, and dumb. Do you have any idea of the beings I have fought and defeated?"

"Me giant problem for you, puny man!" Liverwart threw a haymaker at the man's face, but he turned to mist and reappeared to the giant's left. Liverwart threw a mighty backhand, but Ammarod repeated his last action.

Ammarod *smoked* himself as Liverwart threw a knee and reappeared in the air, somersaulting over the giant's head, punching downward and catching him right on the bridge of the nose. Blood spewed from his face and, blinded by pain, unable to breathe, Liverwart stumbled across the room, tripping over and through a table and swinging punches through the air in all directions.

"I'm sorry you had to get involved in this," Ammarod stomped into the side of Liverwart's right knee, which was at Ammarod's waist level, and the giant crumbled in a crying heap to the floor. "You're only trying to defend a friend, giant, and I admire that…it's more than some would do…but you've stuck your nose in where it doesn't belong. I'll make this as quick and painless as possible."

Ammarod drew his rapier again, but as he moved to strike he felt a feeble hand grab his right ankle. Looking down he noticed the orc he'd bitten with a paralysis bite coming to. He kicked Bum away violently and delivered a heavy boot to his face. However, in his distraction, Liverwart had recovered, grabbing Ammarod by the throat with one hand and throwing him across the room and through a window. As he landed outside, Ammarod could feel a shard of glass embed itself deeply into his shoulder blade. He could still dispatch the giant and orc without much trouble, but he knew the ruckus would soon draw the attention of the townsfolk…he couldn't afford to make a spectacle which could draw a more formidable opponent.

"For now, Laurel," he said under his breath and, in the blink of an eye, he turned to smoke, drifting quickly across the river and into the wilderness.

Chapter 3
Dale

All that was in Dale's mind when he awoke, was how to stop that damn headache. Also, the pain in the little finger of his left hand, where a large thorn had somehow lodged. At least the latter he could fix; he put his teeth to the base of the thorn and yanked it out. His finger still hurt, but that would soon enough ease.

It wasn't even dawn yet; the night sky was still visible through the trees. Dale sat up and examined his surroundings. He had nestled between the exposed tree roots of a mighty cedar, safe within nature's refuge. He'd covered himself with his brown traveler's cloak, making him indistinguishable in the black forest, and had used a thick wadding of moss for a pillow. He was in the north...the foothills...and he was trying to find safe passage into the mountains. He remembered the Kudgel threat, and the Sky Titans, and knew that, while he'd love to continue sleeping on his bed of moss, bugs, and earthworms, his party couldn't afford to waste any time in getting to Alfen Gulfadex. Jumping to his feet, he wrapped his cloak across his torso, tying it in a knot at his hip, fastened his utility belt and sword, and called out to his companions. "Ben, Helena, and purple haired horny toad...time to wake up! We gotta..."

Wait, where the hell was everyone?

He searched high and low in the surrounding woods, calling the names of his companions, but everywhere he went, he just found more trees. He gathered his belongings and wandered about, trying to make sense out of where he was and what had transpired. Dale had always prided himself on his memory, but at this particular moment he was having trouble just remembering the names of his companions. Finding his way to a small brook, he knelt down and dipped his entire head into the icy water. While immersed, he muttered an old incantation taught to him by Cycleze long ago, and as if a lightning bolt had stuck him right in the face, he flew back from the edge of the stream.

"It's all coming back to me..." Dale gasped.

He never liked using the spell, especially not now, since it only worsened his headache. But, of all the spells Cycleze had tried to teach him in years gone by, it was one of the few Dale found practical. Cycleze had a name for the spell, but all Dale bothered to remember about it was that it helped recollect memories that had been lost due to physical trauma, hexes, or other sorts of chemical or magical interference. It didn't bring back all the details, but enough for Dale to know what had happened.

We'd made our way into Upper Sultry, and were ambushed by a group of Kudgels. We were tortured, drugged—which I presume is the reason for my faulty memory—and we were going to soon be killed when, somehow, Benny had gotten loose and freed Helena, Burgundy, and I. We got separated while fleeing; I had to fight off a group of Kudgel soldiers...and I guess wandered around half-conscious until I came to that large tree over yonder.

Dale rubbed his forehead hard while conducting his interior monologue. He wished the incantation had brought back the finer details, such as who (if anyone noteworthy) had lead the Kudgels that caught them, how Benny had gotten free, and how they were separated, as well as how long Dale had been lost in the woods before falling unconscious underneath the tree. Judging by the growth of his beard, Dale suspected he'd been separated from his companions about two weeks, as he did remember shaving on the morning before their capture.

Should've paid more attention to Cyc's teaching, Dale thought. *But he was always by my side, and I thought he always would be. I never needed to learn any magic.*

If he'd been well-practiced with the few spells he knew how to perform, he'd have been able to recall his entire memory, but he had to make do with what he had. It was possible that the particulars would fill in the blanks as time wore on, but there was no telling how long that would be. So, he walked along the shore of the stream until he arrived at a small bridge and trail leading through the woods. It was narrow, but appeared to be somewhat traveled due to the bare ground of the trail; so, judging by the constellations, he took the path leading northwest.

For all his traveling in Lower Sultry, he'd never really explored the northern continent aside from the Imperial City and the surrounding country. From the gently sloping terrain of the forest, he guessed he'd arrived at the foothills of the northern mountains, which began just after the Imperial City and increased in crest and valley until becoming the actual mountain range.

He'd walked for hours, until the sun arose, but even then the trees kept Dale in near darkness. The day dragged on, Dale stopping occasionally to relieve himself and to rest his feet. The headache subsided, and just as Dale could see the red rays of the setting sun through the dense foliage of the forest, he heard the beating of hooves and a loud voice call out from behind him.

"Ho, there!"

"Who the hell are you?" wasn't the response the "golden one" expected out of the disfigured, minuscule southerner, but he obviously hadn't read Dale's resume. The man was small compared to most of Upper Sultry's super-sized royalty, only standing around seven and a half feet tall. But what he lacked in size he made up for in arrogance and brass.

He dismounted from his abnormally large steed and approached Dale.

"I am Lord Leofrickus of Forthwind. I seek the Sages of Knavesmare; does this road lead there?"

Dale shrugged but didn't respond. He couldn't remember a thing about the sages, but the title sounded familiar, so he knew they must have something to do with his quest. If the path at hand did indeed lead to them, why else would Dale have been so close to the trail when waking?

"Well, surely you must have some destination...we're nearly a fortnight's journey from any civilization. Where are you going?" His bushy handlebar mustache twitched as he spoke, the oiled curls glinting in a single beam of sunlight. He snatched off the wide-rimmed traveling hat and tapped the toe of his left boot impatiently on the ground.

"North," Dale said.

"North?" The large Upper Sultrian smirked and nodded at Dale, "I should've expected such an obtuse response from a southern imbecile like you. Do you even know where you are?"

"To be quite honest, pal, not really."

Leofrickus laughed heartily. "Typical! Another one of you dumb country bumpkins thinking you're going to trounce on our soil and rule the world!" He mounted his horse once more and they took off on the trail in full gallop. "If you can't take the heat, stay out of the fire."

Soon, the rider and his extravagant cape and steed were out of sight. Dale normally would have taught the noble a lesson in etiquette, knocking the uppity man's teeth so far down his throat he'd be chewing his own ass out, but since his conversion to good via Virtue's magical bite, he realized that being sidetracked by confrontation of any degree would be both inconvenient and unnecessary to the mission at hand. His goal was no longer bloodshed and mayhem.

He continued along the path for the remainder of the day, and stopped in a small clearing just off the beaten path for the night. He never could sleep well at night, so it wasn't surprising when he heard a twig break in the distance. More noise was made, and he soon could make out distinct footsteps coming towards his small camp beside a tree. As he sensed the figure at his back hovering over him, he reached back, locking his arm around the figure's leg. He kicked up into the air, only his neck and shoulders remaining on the ground as he brought his right heel down in an ax-like chop onto the figure's head. There was a grunt and the figure toppled onto the ground as Dale mounted and captured the small man in an arm bar. Cranking down on the small arm locked between his legs, Dale was about to break it when he heard a familiar voice. "Dammit, Dale, it's me!"

Just then, Dale could make out Burgundy, the dwarf, and his purple hair in the moonlight. "Horny Toad?" He let go. "Then why didn't you say anything, jackass? I was gonna tear you limb from limb. I didn't know what the hell you were!"

"You've been kicking my ass around the whole trip anyway. Every time I so much as looked at Helena you'd boot me in the ass or slap the back of my head!"

"Every night you dry-humped her in your sleep!" Dale yelled.

Burgundy waved his hands to hush Dale down. "Whatever! Whatever! I'm just saying, I wasn't sure if you'd even want me around you after shit got crazy and we split up after the ambush…and I wasn't entirely sure it was you…I'm not about to announce myself to a complete strang…"

"Just shut up, you idiot! I don't want to hear it right now." Dale went back to his bedroll and pulled his cloak back over his body.

Burgundy walked over to where he'd apparently set his traveling gear on the other side of the clearing. "Yeah, good idea. We'll get sleep and deal with things in the morning."

"And if I feel hands on my shoulders and a poke in the rear tonight..." Dale threatened.

"I'm hard up but not that hard up! I ain't queer anyway, and if I was I'd surely pick someone a bit better looking than you! Goodnight, ass face."

"Goodnight, stubby," Dale replied.

The entire camp could tell Kuch the dragon-rider was terrified of the judgment their new leader would bestow upon him for failing to kill the Amazon. Kuch wasn't one to be intimidated easily (how could you scare someone who has tamed a dragon?), but there was so little known about their leader, even gender being left a mystery, and the ethereal power which had been displayed by this entity had brought even the most hardened of Kudgels to their knees. Dragons, trolls, and giants...all of these and more Kuch could handle. But, like most Kudgels, it was the fear of the unknown which had them under this being's power.

Some of the more stubborn members of the camp had doubted the power of their leader at first. After all, why should such a proud race as the Kudgels obey the command of someone who won't even reveal his/herself? They passed off the displays of power as the simple parlor tricks of a novice mage, and even the warnings of the leader's spokesman, the vampire, Ammarod Current, could not quell this lot of upstarts.

That night, a terrible sickness had come down upon the village, but it only affected those who had initially resisted the leader and its spokesman. They came down with fever, their hair fell out, and horrible hives and boils erupted all over their bodies. Then, as if their insides had literally liquefied inside of them, their innards spewed from every orifice: a mash of lung, liver, stomach, heart, and intestines in fecal jelly. Kuch witnessed his brother fall victim to the malady firsthand, and, horrified at the prolonged, torturous death, had submitted himself whole-heartedly to Ammarod and his master.

Today was unique, however, because the leader had requested to see Kuch personally. Nobody, save Ammarod and the Grand Hydra (a high ranking hill giant recruited years past) could enter the leader's private tent. This could only mean one of two things: either he would be rewarded for being the only surviving member of his party, or he would be severely punished for failing to kill the Amazon. As he reached the small, ocher walls of the tent, the green-robed giant turned to Kuch. Normally the Grand Hydra would mock and jeer at one who would face the leader, but he knew and respected Kuch. Kuch was in a class all his own; a special order of elite, pure-blooded Kudgels who were ordained to tame and master the last of the dragons. Kuch was the poster-child of the Kudgel army: hardened, diligent, and defiant until the end. His multi-colored tattoos covered every inch of his body, and his tusks had been ornately carved with images of dragons and inlaid with gold. The scars on his arms marked the number of kills he had achieved, and his loincloth, which Kuch only wore on special occasions, was made from the fur of a saber-toothed tiger, the tail left intact and dangling from his waist at the back. To a member of the Kudgel army, recruit or no, this being demanded respect. The Hydra looked into Kuch's eyes, and gave a somber nod. They both knew the possible outcome of this meeting.

"You may enter," he said.

Kuch stepped through the gauzy curtains, and became immersed in darkness. He was nervous, and began scratching the still raw scar across his chest, and fought off the urge to dig into his wounded thigh. The golden bangles on his arm clanked as he shook with the unnatural cold of the tent, and he looked around until at last a bright candle illumined the room. Aside from the stacks of ancient tomes, and the crystal ball on a small table at the rear of the room, the only other item was a sheet of black cloth, hanging from the ceiling and wrapped around a small figure. Kuch looked around, and was astonished to find no poles supporting the tent; the cloth seemed to support itself.

"Step forward, Kuch," came a voice from within the black cloth. It was deep and unnatural, as if modified to conceal the identity of the thing hidden inside the curtain.

He stepped forward and fell to his knees. "I am frightened by your power, great one, but I will not make excuses...I have failed you."

Laughter filled the tent. It was not maniacal or malevolent. If anything, it seemed eerily kind and reassuring.

"How have you failed me, Kuch?" it asked. "You chased Helena the Amazon for days on end, commanded your troops well, you even survived a duel with Nolan Ducat...yes, I know what has transpired. You need not explain yourself, or be afraid."

"It is true, master. We chased the woman night and day. My troops combed the wilderness, my dragon ravaged the countryside...but I only survived because the one-armed man let me. I was no match for him."

"You're too hard on yourself. Nolan Ducat is a legend...practically a god...he would not have spared your life unless he respected your power. That is something to be proud of."

"You're not going to punish me?" Kuch was perplexed.

"Oh, contraire! You will be rewarded, although it may not feel that way when it comes," it said.

Kuch knew something was up. "I respect your power, but I know when I hear a lie. I've seen your power, and know any defense is futile, but the least you could do is be honest with me, master. What do you plan to do with me?"

"I plan to give you eternal life." Kuch knew he was doomed when he heard those words.

He tried to turn and run, but his feet were held in place. Black mist rolled in from under the walls of the tent, spiraling around Kuch like a tornado, cutting off his air supply as it shot up his nose, in his ears, and down his throat. He gasped for breath, grabbing his neck as he felt the icy grip of death upon his heart, squeezing it like a vice. After the mist had done its job, Kuch was nothing but a mummified husk that shattered into dust as he fell to the ground. As the mist retracted from the pile of gray ash, it took form, feet first, until Ammarod Current stood facing where Kuch had been.

His dark countenance turned upon his master wrapped in the shroud. "It's a shame to lose a skilled rider like Kuch. Many in our army are expendable…he wasn't."

"But you need worthy souls to help you grow strong, and prolong your life. Kuch is now a part of you, his skills, abilities…everything is yours now, just as with the others. Their souls haven't been thrown out like the contents of a bedpan from an upper story window. Do you question my wisdom, child?" the voice asked.

"I question nothing," Ammarod had no fear of the being within the curtain. "But as your child, I have inherited your wisdom. You should know better than I, that even with infinite abilities one can only accomplish so much. Would you have me absorb our finest warriors one by one, until only I am at your disposal?"

"Your opinion is well noted. Now, on other matters…" the voice was obviously annoyed with Ammarod's defiance.

"I was unsuccessful at killing Laurel. She had friends…I'm ashamed to say that being clouded with rage, they got the better of me, and I left before our quarrel drew the attention of the townsfolk. I let pride and vengeance detour me from our prime objective. I will return and…"

"You will do no such thing!" the voice said, "You have been to her twice, the first time taunting and the second to slate your lust. You could have ended this in a second while she slept, but your feelings are and will hinder you from killing her. Your troops also failed to bring in Ben Clout. In fact, they nearly killed him!"

Ammarod dropped to his knee not out of fear, but reverence. "I am sorry. I know how much you desire to have Benny Clout with us…had he died I would have…"

"But he didn't die, did he? In fact, it was just as I thought. Your brother Benny proved to be just as resilient as you were. I will take care of Laurel, my son, and destroy her for tearing apart our family! But we will be reunited once again. You must believe in my power and obey my instructions." The voice slowly changed until the high pitch of a woman filled Ammarod's ears.

A petite, milky white hand reached out from the curtain and its black nails caressed Ammarod's face. He reached out and held it tenderly, kissing it.

"Yes, mother," he whispered.

Chapter 4
Benny

"Wake up, filth!" Benny heard as he was shoved off of his stool and onto the hard floor. "Judgment time has come."

Benny was confused, and there was a bad scrape on his arm. How had he come here?

Picking Benny up by the hair, the guard bound Benny's hands in front of him and dragged him back into the hallway and led him to a staircase. After an eternity, they reached a wooden door, which the guard kicked open, heaving Benny into the blinding sunlight.

"Move, dammit!" A boot kicked him in the butt and shoved him back onto his face.

"Keep knocking me around and I won't go anywhere," Benny snapped.

The Voot responded by delivering a resounding blow to the back of Benny's head. Realizing it was ridiculous to try and resist in his present state, Benny gritted his teeth and allowed the Voot to "escort" him into a large courtyard. Once his eyes had adjusted, Benny realized he was actually in a lush garden, surrounded by a multitude of flora that he'd never seen before. They traversed a narrow stone pathway through the grounds until he arrived at a gazebo where three Voot men sat in ceremonial robes. They were obviously top brass.

"Hello, friend. I trust you've found our facilities accommodating?" the oldest Voot asked.

"Quite," Benny replied.

The oldest Voot motioned for him to sit down on a cushion which had been placed in front of this elder council. His head, like the other tiger-men, was stout and rounded. However, unlike the others Benny had seen of the species, his fur was white striped with black instead of the various striped shades of orange and gold. As he spoke, his canines were exposed, and Benny couldn't help but wonder if the pink staining was from blood. He wore a thick overcoat made of the same silky material Benny's own attire was made out of, except it was far more elaborate, embroidered on a softer white material across the breast of the cloak, with the image of a swan before a setting sun sewn into it. On his head, he wore a tall red hat, rectangular in shape, with a thick cord of red and blue cloth with frilly tassels at the end. The two elders bordering him were dressed in a similar fashion.

"You're probably wondering who we are," the elder motioned to his comrades. "I am Wang, and these two seated beside me are my personal advisers."

"You're the big cheese around here, then?" Benny asked.

The Voot elder chuckled under his breath. "Your colloquialisms are amusing. If by 'big cheese' you mean some type of leader, the answer is yes and no. I am the eldest of our people and, as such, I have been given special privileges and honors, as granted by the election of our people. But I am no king. We are a communal society, young human. We work together, sharing with and living off each other. No one here is any better than the next, myself included. However, under certain circumstances, like your own, one must be chosen to make decisions and determine the fate of certain undesirables. That is where we come in. We would like to know why you are here."

"I don't remember how I got here," Benny said. The elder frowned.

"I can assure you, human, things will be a lot easier on you if you tell the truth. Outsiders do not merely 'stumble' onto our land. When they do, there is *always* a motive."

"For years without number, our race has been on the brink of extinction...we are victims of war and conquest, we have been enslaved, beaten, and massacred...forced into religion, government, and colonization by the race of man, dwarf, and elf...forced to immigrate from our homelands...we have been ravaged by famine and disease..." another elder said before being cut off by the white Voot.

"The list goes on..." he said, "So, you have two choices, human. You can tell us why you are here, in which case we will have mercy on your life, or you can be executed."

"If I tell you why I'm here, you'll let me go?" Benny asked.

The white tiger-man laughed. "We will let you live, but you must remain here. You will be integrated into our society, an indentured servant at first, but through hard work, discipline, and reeducation, we may grant you citizenship in time."

"So you'll do to me what you claim others have done to you?" Benny asked, growing annoyed.

The elder on the left shook his head. "You misunderstand, human. In order to maintain our civilization, tradition states that, should any outsider arrive within our lands, they are to be either killed or integrated into our city. We do this not out of hatred, but because of the hardships our ancestors faced at the hands of races like humans, dwarves, hobbits...we do this for our own safety."

"Are you even listening to what you're saying? You're doing the very thing to me that you CLAIM was done to your people who knows how long ago. You yourselves are admitting these 'atrocities' committed against your people were done long ago, perhaps centuries. Hardly anyone even knows the Voot exist anymore! Until half a year ago, I didn't even know what the Voot were. There may have been some truth to what you're saying, but these are events that happened centuries before the oldest of you today were even born! What documentation do you have of this horrible history?"

"Documentation?" The eldest Voot seemed perplexed by the statement.

Benny rolled his eyes, "I mean how was this history recorded? What proof do you have that any of this stuff even happened?"

"We have the word of our forefathers, passed down through countless generations! Do you accuse our forefathers of being lairs?" The eldest Voot was irate.

"No, I have nothing against the ancestors of your race. I have no clue what happened back then, and I'm not going to make judgments now. But you speak as if the world is out to get you. The world barely knows you exist!" Benny knew angering the elders wasn't wise, but he couldn't believe how hypocritical and ignorant Voot philosophy was.

"Be that as it may." The jovial, inviting grin of the white elder was gone, replaced by a stern, emotionless expression. "We can't risk the utter destruction of our race by letting intruders, malevolent or no, go free."

"I am one human, and barely out of diapers at that." Benny stood up. "And I am being honest when I say I don't remember how I arrived in your land, but I do remember my destination before being separated from my companions. I know I must leave here and get to the Northern Mountains...to Alfen Gulfadex! Your backwards, militaristic, exclusionist society depends on it! The world depends on it! I have to leave here!"

"You speak as if our very existence depends on a whelp of a man like you!" The elders laughed hysterically.

"I don't have time to explain it to you ignorant hicks! If I don't get to Alfen Gulfadex and stop the Kudgel army from summoning the Sky Titans, the entire world will be destroyed. All of Pakk! In the name of the Protector, please let me go!" Benny was frantic.

The White Voot had a look of anger and confusion. "I do not know of these Kudgels, or of Alfen Gulfadex, or the Sky Titans, but I have heard of the deity known to many as the Protector, and all of the ignorant, pathetic beliefs surrounding him. You come here in an attempt to force religion and false doctrine on us…to manipulate us and trick us into conforming to your society. Tell me, did you come up with this story yourself, human? Or did the Emperor have his royal advisers think this little story up for you? Judging from your appearance, I'd argue the latter!"

"I'm not trying to convert you," Benny protested. "Only to make you see the truth."

"Guards, take this hairless worm back into the dungeons!" the elder on the right screamed.

Benny was grabbed under the armpit by the same guard as earlier, and before he was out of earshot heard the voice of the white elder making his final statement. "When your god's dead and forgotten, will he mourn for you?"

Benny's clothes were stripped off him and he was thrown back into the muddy crypt the guard had pulled him from earlier. In the darkness, he heard a gruff voice chuckling, and figured it was the prisoner he'd talked to earlier.

"Go that well, huh?" he said.

"Just about," Benny said. "Join or die."

"Throw that crap at you, too, eh? Die we will, but not by execution…we'll spend the rest of our miserable days in this hellhole. They want to forget about us, not kill us."

Benny looked in the direction of the door. "Is there any way of escaping? How strong is the door? Can it be broken down if enough of us work it over?"

"No way, it's reinforced with steel *and* it's enchanted. Even if you could break through, though, there's a guard just outside. And if you get past him, you have the rest of the dungeon maze to work your way through and countless other soldiers. No, you're pretty much screwed. Make yourself comfortable, kid."

Benny didn't respond, leaning back against the cold stone wall, his bare behind sitting on sparse amounts of hay and some wet substance; he tried not to guess what it was. So he sat in darkness, drifting in and out of sleep; it seemed pointless to try and find a way to escape. *If Dale were here it'd be different*, Benny thought. *He'd use a mage cry and blast his way out…or if Virtue were here she might've given me a strength bite or something.* But "what ifs" didn't mean much when locked in a dungeon. Minutes turned into hours, and hours seemed to turn into days. For all Benny knew, it might have been only a matter of seconds before the door finally opened, but in the darkness it was an eternity. As the door opened, torchlight illuminated the room as a Voot soldier rapidly crossed the threshold and grabbed Benny by the arm. Half asleep, Benny jerked away from him and prepared to fight for his life, thinking his execution near. "Knock it off, you fool, I'm saving your ass!"

"Who are you?"

"I'll explain later." He shoved Benny into the dim corridor, pulling him in the opposite direction the other soldier had taken him earlier. "It's night out and most of the guards are off duty. They don't know I'm doing this, so we gotta act quickly."

"You know a way out?" Benny asked.

"You think I'd be doing this if I didn't?"

They made sharp turns, traversed staircases, and at one point even crawled through a narrow tunnel. The Voot explained on the way that the dungeons Benny had been in were actually the ruins of an older Voot city, which had been built over and converted over the centuries. Only about a tenth of this old city was used for the dungeon, and most of it had been forgotten. "I've been exploring this place most of my life. I know it like the back of my hand, so stay close to me. Once you get lost down here, you'll never get back out." They followed an ancient sewer system, and soon Benny was led to the small entrance, where they traversed a narrow stairway until they reached the outdoors. They came out onto a rocky outcropping on a hill on the edge of the wood, overlooking a small, dirt path.

"Take that path. There's a small human settlement a few hours walk from here. And here, you'll need this…" From a pack on his back, the Voot handed Benny his clothing, weapons, and magic staff. It had to be an enchanted bag, because there was no way all that stuff could have fit inside it, especially the staff and sword.

Benny turned towards the Voot. "Why did you help me?"

"I overheard your conversation with the Elders, and I agreed with a lot of what you were saying. They're stubborn old hypocrites. They've shut us off from the world, and limited our people to the minute confines of our hiding hole. Our civilization was once the center of trade in Upper Sultry…maybe all of Pakk. Now, we are a merely a shard of our former glory: a handful of paranoid fools cowering within our walls. While I'm skeptical of this 'protector' you spoke of, I do know of the Kudgels and the threat they pose, and if you reaching the Northern Mountains will help put an end to their rampage, I want no part in hindering you. I could tell from the tone of your voice you were sincere."

"You're not like the others…seems like you've experienced a lot of this world," Benny stated.

The Voot chuckled. "I have. I discovered at a young age that, while by race I was Voot, my heart was not. I discovered this secret passageway, and ventured many times from our lands. I even managed to compete in the tournament in the Imperial city not long ago."

"I thought you looked familiar. I think you fought my friend Helena, the Amazon. But why are you still here if you dislike it so much? Even now, you could flee this place and never look back."

The Voot shook his head. "Because despite what I feel, they *are* my people…this *is* my home. And it is my duty to protect and guide them. Perhaps if I can one day become an elder, I can guide our people away from the crude, selfish ideologies they now follow. I wish you farewell, and I hope you are reunited with your companions."

They shook hands, and the Voot walked back towards the entrance to the sewers. Benny didn't ask the tiger-man his name, nor did he try to change his mind about the Protector. He'd saved Benny's life, and Benny owed him respect. The Voot's path was his own. Nobody, neither Benny nor the Protector, could walk it for him. He had to find the Protector for himself, in his own way, as Benny had. So, with a silent prayer, he descended the sloping hill towards the dirt trail.

Chapter 5
Helena

"Daddy, let her go!" Noletta screamed.

The cruel grip on Helena's throat paused. "What's it to you, child?" Nolan demanded.

"She's a good woman. Decent company. She treats me like a person. She didn't do nothing to you. She just doesn't know what sets you off. She was just answering your question. Let her be."

"Out of the mouths of children…" Nolan murmured as his grip eased and Helena was able to breathe again.

"'Pologize," Noletta demanded.

Now, the man chuckled under his breath. "As if there were doubt who governs this household." He took a breath. "Helena, I apologize for treating you roughly. You didn't know."

"I didn't know," Helena agreed. But she was learning.

"A while back I had a fling with a pretty girl. Men do, you know. In the morning she went her way and I thought nothing of it. I never even knew her name, just that she was willing and had nice legs." He smiled reminiscently. "Very nice legs. Years later, Dale—yes, you may say his name, now that I've reorganized my priorities—sought me, knowing I was his father. That was when I learned he existed. It was a surprise, nay, a shock, and I reacted badly. I was obsessed with my fame as an adventurer and feared that his presence would prejudice my reputation. I was supposed to be a warrior, not a casual lover! So I shunned him, and he departed."

"May I—" Helena hesitated. "May I express an opinion?" It wasn't that she was afraid of him, for she was taking his measure and knew that she could defend herself against him hereafter if necessary. She was, after all, a warrior, and the same stunts would not catch her again. It was that she was utterly fascinated with what he was saying, filling in key background on Dale, and she didn't want to cause him to stop.

"Sure, we're talking, and you've got a right."

"She's got a right," Noletta agreed.

"It's that he's changed. Virtue Vampire bit him, and he turned from evil to good. He's a different man now, and he's trying to make up for all the damage he did in his bad years. I think you need to know that."

"I do," Nolan agreed. "But that came later. When Dale was older, I regretted turning my back on him. He was, after all, my son. I sought him out and tried to make peace with him. But he was vindictive and refused to accept my apology. I fear that I was part of the reason he became the monster he was. Had I accepted him and taught him the right way to be…" He shook his head. "But it was far too late to undo the way I had hurt him. So I let him be, hoping that he would straighten out on his own, in time."

"He had become radicalized," Helena said. "That's usually a one-way route."

"A dire way," Nolan agreed. "Later, I found out the truth about the Alsbury massacre. That was too much! So, I tracked Dale down and confronted him, telling him that this had to end. But he drew his sword on me. On me, his father! That showed how far he had drifted. I had to put him down. But he had become an excellent swordsman, and it was no easy chore. Yet even in combat, I misjudged him, not actually wanting to hurt him, hoping he would back off. Instead, he grievously smote my arm. It became evident that he had no scruples about trying to kill me. So

I disarmed him—that is, by knocking away his sword—and clubbed him on the head, knocking him out. But I still hesitated to kill him, so I left him, knowing he would survive. He would have to know I could readily have killed him, and maybe that would make him think, and realize how wrong he had gone."

"It didn't," Helena said.

Nolan nodded. "I was foolish to think it would. I just didn't want to believe that my bloodline could veer into evil. Yet I knew I had allowed it, by my prior rejection; there was significant fault in me. The loss of my arm was my penalty for that error. So I removed myself from society, determined to do no further ill. I built my home in the forest and lived alone, a hermit. Until a dryad happened by." Now he smiled reminiscently.

"Dryads can be fetching," Helena said. They were bare nymphs with greenish hair, usually shy around people. If a man were somehow able to catch one, he could do with her what he wished, which was usually only one thing. She noticed that Noletta was paying close, silent attention; this was evidently a subject that interested her.

"They can, indeed. Ordinarily, I would not have been tempted by such a nymph, but Desdemona was different. Her name meant Girl of Sadness, and she was that. She had been rejected by her sister nymphs because she was allergic to oak trees, and of course dryads are creatures of oak. So she took up residence in a white ash tree not far from where I lived. Because she was lonely and she sensed that I was too, she came to me for such limited comfort I could provide. Of course, all I saw at first was her lovely, bare body. I thought she would spook and flee if ever I tried to touch her because my loss of an arm made me ugly. Instead, she wordlessly took my hand in hers. Dryads can talk, but seldom do, at least to mortals. She led me to her tree, and I was surprised that it was not an oak, but it was straight and tall, towering above other trees. She seemed to think that this would make me reject her, but I had no preference for

63

one type of tree over another. 'The ash is a fine tree, with very good hard straight wood,' I said. 'I am glad to have you with it; I know the tree will prosper.' Then she smiled, and kissed me, and led me back to my home, and soon we were lovers."

Helena nodded. "Your arm made you ugly to your kind, and her tree made her ugly to her kind. You had ugliness in common, in the eyes of some others."

"But not to each other," he agreed. "What a delight to me she was, and I think I meant something to her too. Our nights were no longer lonely. I thought I would never love again, but I loved her. She learned to do some housework, and I made sure that nothing molested her tree. I called her my piece of ash, trusting that she did not know my language well enough to pick up on the naughty humor. And in due course she got with child; it turned out that dryads have enough human stock to be inter-fertile with us, if they choose. Perhaps that was her intention, to have a family, since her own kind balked her. I took care of her during her pregnancy, by watering and fertilizing her tree, and finally she birthed Noletta."

"Oh," Helena said, surprised. "Of course." Somehow she had not made that connection before.

"I'm half dryad," Noletta said proudly. "I can't touch oak, but I can do anything with ash. So I'm a chip of ash."

Helena kept a straight face, hoping the child did not know the humor. "And where is Desdemona now? I haven't seen her here."

Both father and daughter suddenly sobered. "Her tall ash tree was struck by lightning in a storm, and it burned to a husk. Mona couldn't exist without it; she faded away. The ash was an ash." He was not smiling. "I salvaged enough of the remaining heartwood to build onto the cabin. Where Noletta and I can sit to feel close to her, and I shaped and polished small pieces for us both." The two of them held up finely grained, egg-shaped slivers, pendants on thin chains around their necks. "It makes us feel closer to her."

Helena was almost sorry she had asked. "I regret bringing up the subject. I did not mean to stir painful memories."

"There's never any pain with Mommy Mona," Noletta said. "We like remembering her. Her spirit is always with us."

"In the pendants!" Helena said.

"Yes," Nolan agreed. "She was always imbued in the tree, and she animates these last pieces of it."

"We kiss her, and she kisses us back," Noletta said.

Surely they were imagining that. "That's nice," Helena said noncommittally.

But the child picked up on her doubt. "We can prove it! Here, kiss the pendant. If she likes you, she'll kiss you."

Nolan nodded. It seemed he shared the fantasy. Both of them really missed the dryad.

"Uh, Amazons have not had much to do with dryads. She probably wouldn't—"

Noletta held the pendant toward her. "Kiss her! You'll see."

What could she do? Helena kissed the pendant.

And it kissed her back. "Oh, my," she said, quietly stunned.

"See! She likes you! She knows you're here to help us."

"Dryads are magical beings," Nolan said. "Her spirit infused the wood of the living tree, and now infuses the remnants. It's small magic, but meaningful for us."

"I see that," Helena agreed. "She did kiss me. I'm sorry I didn't know her."

Nolan looked at his daughter questioningly. Slowly, she nodded. What was in their minds?

Nolan crossed to the white ash panel, where the cabin had been added to. He reached into a small chest there and brought out a third pendant, mounted on a slender chain. He handed it to Noletta.

The child brought it to Helena. "Wear this," she said.

"But I have no connection to Desdemona," she protested. "I was not her friend or relative."

"You are the courier," Nolan said. "It is for Dale. Give it to him. If it accepts him, the mending will begin."

"Oh." Helena bent her head down, and Noletta put the chain over her head so that it became a necklace with the pendant in front. She felt its gentle animation as it touched her skin. "Yes."

"If it kisses him," Noletta explained.

There was a silence. To abate the awkwardness, Helena changed the subject. She looked at a hanging tapestry on a wall. It depicted a tanned youth under a golden sun taking a dragon by the horns. "I have heard of taking a bull by the horns, but a dragon? That's an expedient way to get scorched and killed."

Nolan shrugged. "It was a gift from one of my earliest adventures. Until I killed the dragon earlier this night, I had never actually done it before. Only wrestling them."

"You were a virgin in that respect?" Helena asked, smiling. She felt she had come to know him well enough now to tease him a bit.

"Just because I never killed a dragon before doesn't mean I didn't know how. The villagers who hired me to kill what they thought was a dragon were mistaken. It was actually a red harpy that had been terrorizing their livestock." He went to the tapestry and drew it back. Behind it was a winter scene, set at night, with a scrawny, scraggly haired youth in buckskins being hauled into the air by the talons of a harpy. But he was in the process of sticking it in the breast with a dagger.

"I didn't bother trying to explain the truth," he said. "I was hopelessly vain in my youth, and eager to make a name for myself. While I had done quite a bit of adventuring, most of the accounts of my life were either highly exaggerated or completely made up by myself to make myself famous. Now, I feel very guilty about that, as well as setting a bad example for Dale."

"Well, you were young," Helena said, trying ineffectively to comfort him. "You shouldn't dwell unduly on the past, knowing that you can't change it. I love Dale, but he does the same thing, brooding over the evils he did long ago. I don't condone those evils, but unless there is something positive that can be done today to ameliorate them, what's the point?"

"You say Dale was evil, and changed to good?" Noletta asked.

"I believe he was good, drifted into evil, and then, yes, converted suddenly to good again and was appalled by his prior evil. I did not know him earlier; I met him in the last stage."

"Why did he convert?" Noletta asked.

Helena tried to demur. "I'm not sure we should get into that right now. There's background that you might find tedious."

"He's my half-brother! We're blood related. I want to know."

Helena glanced at Nolan, who shrugged.

Well, if he didn't object, why not? The girl naturally wanted to know about her notorious brother. "Benny fought him, and used his magic to defeat him, but instead of killing him, he had Virtue Vampire bite him."

"A vampire! Is Dale a vampire now?"

Helena smiled. "No, dear. Vampires don't have to convert others to their kind, though they can. Virtue has different kind of bites, and this one was to suppress the evil in Dale and let his good side take over again. Since then, he's been good."

"Virtue Vampire," the child repeated. "She's good?"

"Very good, as her name implies. She's lovely and sweet and my friend. I even helped her survive when she got bad blood, because Amazon blood can counter some things like that. You would like her."

"A vampire! Weird!"

"Vampires differ, as do people. Some are good, some bad. Most are in between, just doing their thing, whatever it is. Didn't your daddy tell you that?"

"Oh, sure. But it's still weird."

"Life can be weird," Helena agreed.

"So what's Dale doing now?"

"He is doing good, wherever he can. He hopes eventually to do more good than he did evil before."

"No, I mean right now."

"Well, I don't know. There's a war on, and we were in a party to save the country of Dan from the ravages of the Kudgels. We were on our way to try to stop the Sky Titans from being summoned by the blowing of the Gold Horn. But the Kudgels ambushed us. We managed to escape, somehow, and—well, that's when you rescued me, Noletta. Dale must have gone in another direction."

"Oh." The child was plainly disappointed.

"From what you say, I should be proud of my son now," Nolan said.

"As he is now," Helena agreed.

"But I'm not ready yet to face him."

Helena glanced at where his arm wasn't. "I understand."

"You will be moving on now."

"Yes. I really appreciate the way you saved me from the Kudgels, and I'm glad to have learned so much more of Dale's background, but I have to locate and rejoin my party. We still need to stop that horn from being blown. Our world is at stake."

"On the morrow."

"The morrow," she agreed.

"I wish you could stay," Noletta said. "You're almost like a mother."

Helena was taken aback. Of course the child missed her mother! But Amazons simply were not mother material. "I...can't stay." She was surprised by how much it pained her to say it.

"I know." The girl's eyes were brimming. "But maybe could you pretend tonight?"

Pretend to be a mother? The idea seemed ludicrous. Yet, what was the alternative? "I can try. I may not be very good at it. I am a warrior woman. I don't—"

She was interrupted as Noletta launched herself into a tearful, flying hug. What could she do except return it? Of course, Amazons didn't shed foolish tears.

Yet in a moment she knew it was possible. It didn't even feel strange.

Beyond Noletta, she saw Nolan tapping his pendant. Oh, he was letting her know that her mood was because of the one she was wearing for now. Desdemona's spirit was with her, and possibly influencing her reactions. There was no evil in it. The dryad, too, wanted her daughter to have some female company.

The day passed in homelike routine. Helena held the child's hand, and read to her, and walked with her through the surrounding gardens. It was routine, yet fun. Each flower had its story, and each buzzing bee. This was Noletta's world. In the Amazon sense, it was a waste of time, but in the mother sense, it was the stuff of life itself. She knew then that once the war was over, she wanted to assume this role and have her own child. Dale would cooperate, or else.

Nolan and Noletta prepared dinner, with Helena sort of tagging ineffectively along. She didn't know this household, and even had she known where everything was, she couldn't have been much shakes at actually making a family meal. But Noletta pretended that she was following Helena's directions, and so, amazingly, did Nolan. She realized that he, too, missed the family routine. But mainly he was doing it for his daughter. The child was happy, and her feeling radiated to animate them both.

It might all be play acting, but it fostered an unfamiliar emotion: contentment. Helena discovered that she actually liked this pretense of being a woman instead of a warrior. A mother instead of a calculating female. When Noletta found an ant wandering on her wrist, Helena carefully took it off and put it on a shrub in the garden, unhurt. Every little thing counted. This was life, not death.

Nolan brought her a small scroll. "You will need this."

Curious, she took it and unrolled it. It was a detailed map of the area. She would be able to find her way without faltering. "This is invaluable," she said, gratified. "Thank you."

"You have a world to save," he said gruffly. It seemed he simply didn't know how to accept honest appreciation.

That night Helena slept beside Noletta, holding her hand. As she lay on her back, she felt her heart beating. No, it wasn't hers; it was from the pendant on her chest, a gentle, measured pattern. Desdemona! The spirit of the dryad must be pleased. That moved Helena in yet another way.

In the morning she found herself better refreshed than in days. Mother sleep was good sleep.

Then, seemingly suddenly, it was time to go. Helena donned her armor and weapons and stood somewhat awkwardly, not clear how to handle this kind of parting.

"Kiss me goodbye," Noletta said.

Oh. She bent down and kissed the child on the forehead.

"Kiss Daddy too."

Just as the real mother would. But this was hardly appropriate. She opened her mouth to explain, but paused as she saw Noletta's face start to cloud. Could she pretend just a little longer?

She looked at Nolan. He spread his hand, evidently feeling similarly awkward. They were not a couple, but how could they disappoint the child?

She stepped into him, put her arms around him, and delivered a token kiss. But the moment their lips touched there was a pulse from the pendant that sent a warm wave up through her bosom, her neck, her face, and her mouth. Then she was kissing him with phenomenal passion. She knew that his pendant was animating him similarly.

Tokenism be damned; this was Desdemona borrowing her body to smooch her beloved.

"Oh, Mommy," Noletta said, delighted. "Naughty girl!"

On target. But Helena couldn't stop it. She had to deliver every pulse and nuance of the dryad's kiss. It was the desperation of a woodland creature in love.

At last, they fell apart, breathing hard. Helena knew her face was flushed. So was Nolan's.

"That was Mona's kiss," he said, amazed.

"It was," she agreed.

"You can't give away her pendant now," Noletta said. "It fits you too well."

"But it is for Dale!" Helena said.

"You need another." Noletta ran to the little chest and brought out another pendant on a chain. She presented it to Helena, who tucked it into a pocket.

Then she spun about and marched away. She had to, because if she stayed any longer she would never be able to leave.

"When Dale needs me," Nolan called, "I'll be there."

Helena nodded without turning. She could not afford to stop now.

She passed the dead, white ash tree. It was only a tall stump surrounded by white ashes. Of course. She reached out to touch the stump, and felt a pulse from the pendant. It knew.

Then she walked on.

Chapter 6
Dale

Dale was not really thrilled to have the lustful purple-haired dwarf as his traveling companion, but any company was better than none, and he knew that Burgundy would not try to stab him in his sleep.

However, he had one serious reservation. "When you sleep, you dream," he said as they started walking. The dwarf's legs were short, but he could move right along.

"I do," Burgundy agreed.

"Of a beautiful woman who would not touch you in real life, but in your fancy she is all yours, all night."

"Yes. When I run out of lovely women—I don't like to repeat myself too soon—I may dream of men. They can be interesting too."

"Exactly. Don't dream of me."

The dwarf balked. "You can't tell me who not to dream of."

"Yes I can."

"How?"

"I can sense who you are dreaming of. If you dream of me, I will pick you up and hurl you into a tree."

Burgundy nodded. "Your argument is persuasive. So I'll dream of your partner, the lovely Amazon."

"Her neither. Do you think I'll want to clasp her, knowing she's been hopelessly soiled by your dirty dream?"

"Well, then the vampire. I dreamed of her before, and she was most obliging. Truly lovely creature, inside and out."

"No. You've had her; do not smirch her again. She is far too good for you."

"Who, then? I need a pretty one or I don't sleep well."

Dale considered. "Maybe Magenta. She's lovely and experienced. She was a prostitute, and quite skilled, I understand. Now, she's a leader of the Kudgels, guiding them to stop their murderous ways and became good citizens again."

Burgundy nodded. "Does that name suggest her color, as mine does mine?"

"Yes. Her body is attractive green. Her face, hands, feet, and hair are purple, and her eyes are green. That might sound ugly, but she is about as lovely a creature as you will ever encounter."

"She sounds ideal. I will dream of her."

Dale hoped that Magenta would not be wroth if she ever learned, not because of the sex, but because she had not been asked permission and got no recompense.

They made good progress, and camped beside a tall, white ash tree. Dale had an eerie feeling of familiarity for no reason he could fathom; he had no particular association with this type of tree. Yet somehow he thought one might be in his future, in some peripheral manner. At any rate, there was no hostility, no warning of danger; it was just a passing impression.

Burgundy was soon asleep, smiling as he addressed the green and purple lady of his dream. Again, Dale felt a tiny twinge of guilt for his part in her obscure debasement.

As they resumed walking the next morning, it occurred to Dale that the dwarf might have some useful information. "What do you know about the sages of Knavesmare?"

"Not a lot," the dwarf admitted. "Just that they are the last of an ancient civilization, one of the first races created by the Protector. They were the ancestors to humans, dwarves, and halflings. Also, aside from those folk who actually live in the Northern Mountains, they alone know the safe passage to Alfen Gulfadex."

"The route is not safe?" Dale asked, troubled.

"It's the holy city of the frost dwarves," Burgundy said. "Of course it's not readily accessible to the riffraff. Even I don't know how to get there."

"I thought we could find it just by going north and being alert."

Burgundy laughed. "And you're not even a dwarf! What do you think is there for you?"

"I think we need to get there to reunify our party," Dale said. "We'll never find each other wandering randomly around the countryside. I knew it might be a difficult journey, but I've handled those before. What's so bad about the route?"

"I don't know the specifics. Just that anyone who tries to go there by foot winds up either lost or dead. I didn't know you had that city in mind. You'd better pick another place."

Dale had not anticipated this complication. But there might be an answer. "Unless the sages help us."

"You want to jump from the pan to the fire? Stay away from the sages! Just go somewhere else to meet. Your friends will come to the same conclusion."

"No. I think Alfen Gulfadex is best."

"Have I mentioned lately that sometimes you make a stubborn pig seem wishy-washy?"

"Not lately," Dale said, smiling.

The dwarf shrugged. "It's your funeral. And mine. It isn't as if my life is worth much anyway. I don't have an Amazon in my bed at night."

"Lucky for her."

"Well, the castle of the sages isn't far from here."

"You've been there?"

"Not remotely close. I don't even know what it looks like. I just know it's in this area, and we'll know it when you see it."

"*How* will we know it?"

"I have no idea. Only that anyone who sees it knows it."

That didn't seem like much help, but it would have to do. They kept walking.

In due course, they reached the castle of the sages. And paused, impressed.

It seemed to be fashioned of giant, rolled scrolls. They even had inked words on their surfaces. Four of them were standing endwise on the ground, each several hundred feet tall. They looked like windowless towers, except that they were clearly made of thick parchment coiled like huge manuscripts. They *were* huge manuscripts. A giant might pick one up and unroll it to read the text. As it was, only a few words were visible in the aperture, in some archaic script. Perhaps the words were magic, to give the parchment the strength and stability necessary to match the strength of a true tower.

But that was just the supports. Above them hung a much larger rolled scroll, horizontal, evidently held in place by the vertical ones. Except for one detail: they did not touch. There was about fifty feet between the outer portion of it and the tops of the lesser ones.

They stood there and gazed, half mesmerized by the sight. "You did say we'd know it when we saw it," Dale murmured.

"I didn't really believe it," Burgundy said, plainly awed.

"Where are the guards?" For there appeared to be no troops defending the castle. Even the most massive edifice was useless if not defended.

"Maybe it's empty?" the dwarf hazarded. "They moved and left it behind?"

They paused one breath, then both burst out laughing. No, this would not be undefended. The guards would be there, just hidden.

"Well, let's find out." Dale marched forward, his hands clamped on his head to show he wasn't attacking. Burgundy matched him. No one fooled with a defended castle. "Ho, Sages! We come in peace. We seek your advice."

There was no response. The castle did indeed seem empty.

"I don't believe it," Dale muttered.

"Some kind of trick?"

"Why would they bother? We're just passing travelers, of no importance. They don't need to trick us. There must be something we don't properly understand."

They studied the edge of the manuscript that opened almost like a door. Dale tried to read the script on it that seemed to be a line of text extending from the ground up toward the top, but couldn't decipher its mystery.

"That's odd," the dwarf said.

"The whole thing is odd!"

"No, there's a picture painted behind the lines of text. It looks like a stairway."

Dale looked, and saw it. It was so realistic that he almost wanted to put his foot on the bottom step and enter the picture. Which was, of course, crazy.

Burgundy lifted one foot high and set it on the top of the step. Then he heaved himself up and stood on it. "I don't dare look down," he said. "Am I doing what I think I'm doing?"

"You're standing on the bottom step of the stairway," Dale said. "Which is crazy, because it's only painted on. You should be falling to the ground."

"That's what I thought." He took a deep breath. "Are you coming?"

This was impossible, yet there it was. Magic.

Dale lifted a foot and placed it on the step beside the dwarf's feet. It was firm and level. He lifted his hind foot and brought it up to join the first. Now he was standing on the painted step, a foot above the ground. He wasn't in the picture, just on the stair.

How could this be? He decided not to question it. Evidently, the sages had their magic and their ways. They didn't need armed guards.

They mounted the circular stairway side by side, the dwarf struggling but managing. They came to a painted landing about a quarter of the way up inside the scroll tower, Dale judged. There, some unintelligible writing appeared on the parchment wall.

Then, intelligible writing appeared on the wall before them. *ANSWER, EACH: if a man spits on you, how do you respond?*

"I put my hand on my sword and ask him to explain himself," Dale said.

"I kick him in the shin," Burgundy said.

A sluice of water descended the tube. It caught the dwarf and washed him out, literally. He was carried down and to the ground, while Dale stood frozen, unable to help him, untouched by the flow. He could see below and around just far enough to know that Burgundy wasn't hurt, merely soaked and scared. Burgundy scrambled back to his feet and up the painted stairs, climbing back toward the landing.

Meanwhile, new writing appeared on the wall. *The man explains himself: there was a deadly chimera gnat on your collar that the spit swept off before it could bite your neck. He saved your life.*

"I'm glad I asked!" Dale said. Over the years of his travels and combat, he had learned caution; not everything was as it first seemed.

Burgundy returned to the platform. He had caught on that the washout was more of a warning than a punishment. "Where did I go wrong?" he asked. "I answered honestly."

You did, but it was a bad answer. You should have been more cautious.

"Got it. Thank you."

That was it. They had been given a demonstration of the requirements. Honesty and caution. Also, the power of the sages' defense. Dale was impressed.

They resumed climbing the stairway. There were no further challenges.

They came to the top of the scroll. It was level, the parchment coiled tightly enough so as to provide them footing. Above them, the larger scroll floated. That had to be where the sages were. How were they to reach it?

"Maybe the supports are invisible," Burgundy said.

"Maybe so," Dale agreed. "Then we could climb them."

They walked around the top of the tower scroll, but found no invisible bars or wires. There was, however, a pile of tangled cords. They checked these and discovered that they were actually a rope ladder. Aha!

"I'll hurl it up to hang on the bottom of the scroll," Dale said. "Then we can climb it."

"Yes," Burgundy said nervously. "And hope it doesn't drop us halfway there. It's a long way to the ground."

It was indeed. "Honesty and caution," Dale reminded him.

"Got it."

They straightened out the ladder, which did seem to be long enough. Then, Dale hurled it up toward the horizontal scroll, uncertain how it could catch. But it did catch, maybe on an invisible hook. Dale tugged at it and found it firm. The bottom anchored similarly at the edge of the tower. If this was a challenge to see whether they could figure out how to proceed, they were passing it.

"We may get another question halfway up," Dale said. "I think this one won't be a token demonstration. If either of us misses, we're both dead."

"Got it," the dwarf repeated grimly.

"Then follow me." Dale put his hands on two rungs and started climbing with his feet. Burgundy followed, again struggling but managing.

In a moment, they were out over the ground between the scroll towers. "Don't look down," Dale advised Burgundy.

"My eyes are closed."

When they were about halfway to the big scroll, Dale grabbed for the next rung, and missed. Surprised, he looked. The rung was there, but when he tried again, his hand passed through it. It was illusion.

"Hey!" the dwarf exclaimed below him. "Where's the rung?"

"I think we are at another test," Dale said. "There was a rung when I passed that section, and now there's no rung ahead of me."

"So what do we do?"

"We inquire." He took a breath. "Oh, spirit of the ladder, what do you wish of us?"

A bodiless voice responded. "If a man who wasn't there calls you a coward because you retreated before an enemy force, as you did not, how do you respond?"

Burgundy answered first. "I tell him—" Then he paused, remembering caution. Calling the man a liar would not be productive. "That maybe he misunderstood the report, because we did not retreat."

There was no response. Dale realized this was because only one of them had answered. He took his turn. "I explain that his information is incorrect. We stood our ground, and the enemy thought the better of it and backed off."

"And if he then calls you a liar and threatens you with his sword?"

Dale was angry at the implication, but maintained his caution. "If he refuses to heed the truth, then he is the liar. If he is a liar, he may be a coward himself, trying to transfer his guilt to me. He is bluffing. I will push on past him, knowing that he lacks the gumption to attack me, because he knows I will smite him if given cause."

Then he put his hand back on the phantom rung, and it was solid. He forged on up the ladder.

"I'm with Dale," the dwarf said, and followed, his rung also back. Then, under his breath, he said "I'm glad he didn't ask me what I'd do about a beautiful woman who called me an ugly little monster and wouldn't let me touch her."

Dale smiled. That woman would get a thorough reaming in dreamland.

They reached the scroll and climbed onto its lower edge. There was a platform leading into a chamber with a door on the far wall. A man was there, facing the door. Dale recognized him: the arrogant Lord Leofrickus of Forthwind, whom he had encountered on the way here. "Hello, Lord Leo," he said.

The man turned. He was in ceremonial garb, with tight, black trousers and an encompassing, silver coat that reached to his knees. Every button shone. "Oh, so you made it, peon. You and your runty, discolored friend."

Burgundy opened his mouth, but closed it from caution, remaining silent.

"So nice to see you again," Dale said with careful irony.

"Just stay out of my way. The sages will soon make short work of you. Your kind doesn't belong here."

"How so?" Dale kept his voice neutral, though the Upper Sultrian Royal was exactly the sort that they had encountered in the question on the ladder. Did he represent another test of their patience?

"Don't you know the first thing about the sages, you moron? They share their information only at a price. Any supplicant must enter a hypnotic state where he will relive one of his worst acts. If he is pure of spirit and good of heart he will remain sane after the vision and will be granted safe passage. If he is naturally vain, evil, malignant, or whatever, he will become insane, haunted by his atrocities for the rest of his miserable life. So you can see that you two oafs should scramble back down the ladder right now; at least you'll save whatever there is of your dull minds."

"Thank you," Dale said with perfect sincerity. "This is valuable information."

"As I said, your kind doesn't belong here. You are best off to accept your lowly place and not aspire to unreasonable heights."

"We will consider your advice carefully," Dale said.

The door opened. A monk appeared, wearing a modest brown robe. "Ah, there's my turn," Lord Leofrickus said, and marched through without even asking the monk. The man quietly closed the door behind him.

"Phew!" Burgundy said. "I almost exploded, holding back my outrage. What an ass!"

Dale nodded. "If his kind is what the sages want, we are, indeed, doomed."

"I spend a lot of time dreaming, as you know. But I do know the difference between a dream and reality. That man is living in a dream."

"We all do, to an extent," Dale agreed. "And yes, most of us know the distinction. But we really don't know what the sages are like. They could be like Leofrickus."

"If they are, we are doomed."

The door opened again. The monk stood there.

"You or me?" Dale asked the dwarf.

"You next. If you go crazy, I'll know there's no hope for me, and will follow Lord Frick-Ass's advice and get out of here."

"I hope to see you again soon," Dale said. He bowed his head briefly to the monk, who silently returned the gesture of respect. "I am ready, if you will be so kind as to conduct me to my interview."

The monk nodded, and they walked into the next chamber.

The sages were seated around the room, facing the center where Dale stood. They did not speak aloud. All were shrouded in voluminous, gray capes with hoods so that he could not see their faces.

He heard a moan. There to the side, lying on a pallet, was Lord Leofrickus, hunched in a fetal position, weeping. "Mother, mother, forgive me!" he cried. He seemed to have lost his sanity.

Dale hardly cared about the arrogant man, who surely deserved to suffer. But why did he remain here, instead of being secluded in a private cell to suffer in peace?

Why else? To show Dale the penalty for failure. This was no child's game. He could still back off.

Except that he still saw no better way to pursue his mission than to go to Alfen Gulfadex. He faced the capes.

Welcome, traveler. What can we do for you?

Oh. They were speaking in his mind.

"I am glad to meet you at last," Dale said politely. "I wish to obtain safe passage to Alfen Gulfadex for myself and my companion."

You choose a difficult manner to travel there.

"We have become separated, and our mission is important. I must travel in the manner that avails me."

One of the cloaked figures lifted a hand and pushed back the hood to reveal the head. Lo, it was a beautiful woman! Her hair was a brilliant, pale yellow shroud that framed her face like an ornate picture frame. That face was so perfect in its contour and symmetry that he found it difficult to gaze directly at it. The eyes mirrored the hair, large, yellow orbs that were hypnotic in their compelling focus.

For the moment, Dale was taken aback. He was not sure what he had expected of the sages, but certainly it was not any female, even a less lovely one.

"Please," he said candidly. "I will not be able to assimilate what you say to me if I am gazing at your rapturous beauty. I was not prepared for such a view."

You may not select my aspect. I will show you what I choose. She stood, and began to open the front of her cape.

"I apologize!" Dale said quickly. "I merely meant that I am ill equipped to process such phenomenal pulchritude. You risk wasting your own time by distracting me."

The sage paused, then drew her cape back together. Then, she sat back down, and drew her hood up to conceal her hair and face. It seemed that she accepted his apology.

Another sage pushed back her hood. This one had deep red hair, the color of blood, and a face that was different in detail but every bit as lovely as the first. Her red eyes fixed on him. *You do not wish to gaze upon our features?*

"I am married," Dale said desperately. "Your features threaten to alienate me from my wife. I'm sure this is not your intention."

Aptly put. She drew her hood back to put her face in the shade.

A third sage opened her hood. This one's hair was lustrous brown, and her eyes matched. She was, if anything, even lovelier than the other two. *And if the price of our cooperation is your cooperation in bed?*

He realized that they were teasing him. "Please, lustrous ladies. It would be another form of insanity from which I might never escape. I acknowledge your power, and beg you to spare me."

The third sage closed her hood. *You must understand the severity of the vision you will suffer. You could be in torment for the rest of your life. Not even one of us could extract you from it.* Her eyes flicked briefly toward the suffering Upper Sultrian.

"I believe it," Dale said. "Yet, if this is the price of your assistance, I must risk it. I will accept whatever happens, because there are more important things at stake than my sanity."

Such as?

"Such as the salvation of our world."

May we verify this in your mind?

"Yes." As if he had a choice.

Then, their minds entered his, with a curious twisting evocation that was both frightening and unutterably pleasant. The lines of their exploration slid into his most private places, laying him mentally bare. It was like penetrating a woman, only the women were penetrating him. They could do whatever they desired with him, and he lacked both the power and the will to deny them.

Then, their passionate threads withdrew, leaving him both relieved and heartbroken. *It is true.*

"Thank you," he said, finding himself intact again.

A fourth sage opened her hood. Her hair was as black as midnight, with tiny stars sparkling in its recesses. *Your case seems worthy. Have you any questions?*

"Nothing of substance. Only curiosity."

She smiled, and it was like soft moonlight in the shadow. *Ask.*

"Frankly, I expected males. Why are all of you female?" He could tell by their svelte outlines, now that he was alert to the signs, that all of them were women.

The black-haired sage frowned, and it was like a velvet curtain shrouding the glow. *Our men have better things to do than dally with incidental travelers.*

Oh. So this was mere scut work. "Thank you."

You will enter the vision when you are ready.

"I'm ready now. Ready as I'll ever be."

Dale found himself in a young version: large, muscled, with short, spiky hair on top and long hair in dreadlocks hanging down his back. He was wearing a blue and white striped tunic, several outlandish weapons, and a red phoenix feather tied into his hair. He remembered the feather as a gift from his former friend, Cycleze, to give him supernatural speed and agility in battle.

He looked around. He was in a swamp, confronting a group of his rival mercenaries, who were led by the Butternut brothers.

"You stole a hit meant for us!" Bruno Butternut accused him.

Now he saw a large slug, with his sword sticking out of its head portion, lying at his feet. He was obviously guilty, as this swamp was their working territory.

But he bluffed it out. "I go where I go, do what I do."

"Yeah?"

"Yeah."

Another Butternut was sneaking around behind him. That was Buddy, who did the dirty work dictated by his big brother. Dale was aware, but pretended not to be. He could handle this situation, but preferred to have a pretext to justify his response before he acted.

A hand grasped his hair, and a knife came to touch his throat. But Buddy was inexperienced, not the knife fighter Dale was. He had not broken his victim's balance, and that was mischief, as he might soon learn the hard way.

"Yeah?" Bruno asked again.

"If you're going to kill me," Dale said evenly, "do it now, because if you don't, I'll take that knife from your lackey. Except."

"Except what?" Bruno asked. He was the talker in his family, and he liked toying with his victims, as Dale knew and counted on.

"Except that when I do, I'm gonna rape him with it, then you, and then I'll rape your brothers and all your friends. Especially your girl."

Bruno burst out laughing, and his gang echoed him. Including Buddy. That was the key.

Dale went berserk, but there was method in it. One hand came up to block Buddy's knife hand as Dale twisted his neck away and clear. Then his other hand cracked down on the youth's wrist, breaking it. He took the knife from the flaccid fingers and swept it across Buddy's throat. Buddy was dead while still standing, not yet aware of his passing.

Dale stopped clear of the falling corpse before the blood could spatter him, whirled, and plunged the blade into Bruno's groin. That man, too, was effectively dead before he realized it.

Then, Dale tackled the other members of the gang, slashing them before they reacted to the astonishing change in the situation. It was a battle of blood, steel, and fire, except that it was really more of a slaughter than a fight. In moments, all were dead or dying except one.

That one was Bruno's moll, Trista, a pretty girl in a red skirt who went wherever Bruno did, always ready to oblige him. She, at least, had time to appreciate the devastation around her. "Don't kill me, please!" she begged tearfully.

Dale bore her to the ground and opened his pants without dropping the bloodstained knife. He felt up under her skirt and ripped away her panties. He didn't bother to kiss her. He raped her, and she didn't resist, knowing that death was the alternative. He had always had the hots for her, but couldn't touch her because of the gang. Now he had her.

Sated, but not yet withdrawing, he brought the knife up before her face, making sure she saw it. Trista's eyes widened in terror as she understood his intention. He slashed her throat, and felt her tighten around him as she died. Then, at last, he withdrew and stood up, his frenzy abating.

One more detail. He dragged the bodies into a pile, then picked up Trista, ripped away her clothing, and dumped her on top, naked, her face staring at the sky, her legs widely spread. When the other members of that gang who had not been here came, they would find an ugly memorial.

He tied his leggings and walked away from the grisly pile. His job here was done.

Dale came to, horrified, begging for forgiveness, but sane.

Forgiveness for what? a new sage inquired. Her hair was gray, signifying age, but she remained outstandingly lovely.

"For my brutality. I deliberately provoked the encounter because I had a grudge against the Butternuts, so I could slaughter them. I did it just because I could. I had no conscience, no mercy. Trista especially; she would have stayed with me, become my moll, because she had little will of her own. I had especially no reason to hurt her. Yet I raped her and killed her, giving her no chance."

Can you forgive yourself?

"No," Dale said. "That's why it haunts me."

What have you done about it?

"I have tried, since my conversion, to do enough good to make up for the evil I did before. I still have a long way

86

to go. I will keep at it until I die. But I don't see how I can ever make up for that one. As I said, Trista haunts me."

Turn around.

Were they dismissing him? So be it. Dale turned around.

There stood a woman of about his own age, unremarkable except for one thing that made his jaw drop.

It was Trista.

"But I killed you!" he said.

"No, you did not. You did not even rape me. You told me that I did not belong with a gang, and I should go far away and find a new life. Then you departed."

"But I remember!"

"Your memory is false. Maybe it came upon you years later, a product of your guilt about many crimes you committed. But me, you spared. I knew, then, what I know now: there was always a bit of good in your core, the center of your being."

Now, Dale began to remember. It was true; he had not actually committed that particular rape and killing. But it fit so well with his bad life that it had become real to him.

"Trista—where did you go?"

She smiled. It did not light up the chamber; she was pretty but not beautiful. "I went to the sages to ask their advice. They took me in, and I became a housemaid for them." She smiled again. "Such chores are necessary things, even among the exalted, and the work is steady. I have never gone hungry or been brutalized again. My name means 'girl of sorrow,' but I am reasonably happy here. It's much better than traveling with a gang. I was raped many times before I came here, just not by you. Your advice to me was good."

"I am glad," Dale said sincerely. "Not about the rapes. About your happiness." Then he turned back to the Sages. "You saw me coming! You knew about that awful incident."

We knew, the gray haired sage agreed. *We are granting you and your companion passage to Alfen Gulfadex.*

Dale bowed his head. "Thank you."

There was no response. They had tuned him out. Only Trista remained, as it were. "Farewell," she said. Then she walked away.

Chapter 7
Benny

Benny walked for a day and a night from the outcropping where the Voot had shown him the escape from the dungeons. He did not know how he would rejoin his companions; indeed, he could not remember how they had become separated. But at least he was free to search for them.

He finally came to the small village the path served. It looked undistinguished, not a great place to learn much. He was disappointed and frustrated. So, the first thing he did was go to the local tavern and begin drinking. He knew this was not the best procedure—in fact, it was probably downright foolish—but at least it would dull his mind for a few hours. Maybe something would occur to him. Or maybe he would get lucky and run into someone he knew. Away from his friends, and especially away from Virtue, he felt unmoored. He needed her steadying influence in his life.

Damn that raid, or whatever it was that broke up their party! They had important business to accomplish, a world to save, and here he was, floundering alone among strangers. It was probably no better for the others, assuming they still lived. He veered away from that thought; they *had* to be alive! Regardless, it was endlessly aggravating.

A new party barged into the tavern, demanding the best ale. Benny felt a shiver. One of those voices was somehow familiar. Where had he encountered that man before? It was not a pleasant association. But he kept quiet, because even when on the way to getting drunk he knew better than to tip his hand too early. He needed to know what he was up against before he got into a fracas.

Then, the man recognized him. "Benny! Benny the Boob!" he exclaimed. "So we meet again. Don't pretend you don't know me. Onion Belasco, Elf Warrior Extraordinaire! Congratulations on escaping the bear trap!" It was larded-on sarcasm, but it did one invaluable thing: it gave Benny a memory flashback. Suddenly, he remembered what had been blocked before.

The companions had just passed into the border of Upper Sultry: Benny, Dale, Helena, and Burgundy, sharing stories from their past. They were passing through a narrow gorge, left by a temporary river during flood season, harmless in the dry season.

"My mother died at a young age," Dale said. "My father abandoned me. I was adopted by the Beranger family. They—"

"What's that noise?" Helena asked, glancing up. She was generally the most alert to the environment. But before they could react, nets came whirling over the upper contours of the gorge from either side, dropping on them. Then they were fallen upon by Kudgel soldiers. They had somehow blundered into an ambush!

They fought, but were overwhelmed by dozens of soldiers who used the ropes and nets to entangle them and their weapons so that, soon, they were hopelessly caught. The object was evidently capture rather than slaughter. They were unable to prevent the Kudgels from thoroughly trussing them up. They were helpless.

Now, they were hauled before an elf mercenary and his henchmen. "Onion!" Dale exclaimed, recognizing him. "Onion Belasco."

"The same, scarface," the elf said. "Times change, eh?"

"How did you catch us?" Dale asked. "We told no one what our specific route was."

Onion laughed. "We tracked you throughout, idiot. We spread attractive magic beacons about, of special interest to dwarves, knowing that eventually one would be found and picked up."

"Damn!" Burgundy said. He managed to pull a bright bead from his pocket and drop it to the ground before him. "I should have known it wasn't just lying there!"

"You should have, moron," the elf said. "But you were never the sharpest arrow in the quiver, were you? We tracked you, and thus your party, from afar, until we saw where your route had to be. Right through the gorge! Where we could lie in wait without making a sound. It was ideal."

"I heard you breathing," Helena said.

"Sharp hearing, barbarian squaw! But too late, eh? We'll make good use of you, once we get that armor off your torso and put a mail hood over your face so you can't bite. But first, we have to interview the four of you. Business before pleasure, you know."

Helena was silent, knowing as they all did that "interview" was a euphemism for torture. Rape was the least of the ordeals they faced.

Onion eyed Dale. "Not so big, now that Cycleze is no longer here to hold your leash or get you out of sticky situations you blunder into, eh, big boy?"

Dale did not answer.

"Now that Marty is a hopeless drunk, and Laughing Jack's no longer laughing." He was obviously trying to goad Dale into a response so he could rub it in further. "In fact, now that Jack, who was once a long-haired, loud-mouthed dandy, died a fat, bald cripple."

Benny clenched his teeth. This was a monstrously unfair characterization. But Dale held firm. There was nothing to be gained by trying to argue.

"The Ferocious Four are no more! You're the last man standing." Onion continued, facing Dale. "But not for long." His smile was ugly.

The Kudgels efficiently carried them to a tent where they were dumped, bound by hands and feet. There they were left.

This was Interrogation 101: leave the prisoners alone together and let them talk in seeming privacy, perhaps divulging key information. They all knew better than to oblige.

"Why are they waiting?" Benny asked, speaking for the hidden listeners.

"There must be a higher-up on the way," Dale said. "Onion is just a glorified messenger boy. He's waiting for further orders."

This was Response 101: insult the captors while letting no useful information slip out.

"Where do you know him from?" Helena asked Dale.

"Once upon a time we were the Ferocious Four," Dale said. "Onion wanted to join us, but he was never quite good enough to be one of the boys. We held him in contempt, and he knew it. Now he figures to get even, which he could never do on his own. Such quislings can be valuable to their betters in the enemy camp." He smiled. "Until their usefulness ends; then, of course, they are dispatched."

Take that, Onion!

"Did you notice," Burgundy said, "that Onion took off on Helena and Dale, but not Benny or me? I'm beneath notice, but Benny isn't."

"We don't know each other," Benny said.

"He's right," Helena said. "Onion studiously never looked directly at you. He surely at least knows *of* you. He should have taken off on you too."

"Almost as if he is afraid of you," Dale said.

Benny realized it was true. Onion had never met his gaze. Sometimes, what wasn't said was more important than what was said. He shrugged. "Maybe he'll get to me in due course."

"There's a minor mystery here," Helena said.

Soon, they were hustled out to meet that higher-up. This turned out to be a Kudgel with an odd, blue tint to his complexion. He was a fine figure of that type of man, wearing an elaborate, blue robe, shiny blue boots, and a headdress that resembled a blue crown. His face was almost handsome despite his species, as if transformed by the dominating spirit within. This was indeed a leader. Benny was impressed by his lordly demeanor despite hating what he stood for. "Do you know me?" he asked them.

None of them did. They looked blankly at him.

"Oh, I forgot," he said. "I'm wearing a new body. Well, I will introduce myself. I am Ammarod Current. I and my superior are taking over where the Grand Cyclops left off. Perhaps I owe you a favor for taking him out."

They remained silent, mainly from caution. Favor or not, he was not their friend.

"Feel free to speak," Current said. "It will not affect your treatment. You are slated to be tortured regardless."

Some reassurance!

"Very well," Helena said. "I am no fan of the Grand Cyclops, though I knew him as a gentleman named Purp. I do respect his sister Magenta, who is a fine, if colorful, person. But he and his ilk would be no match for the four of us in a fair fight. For that matter, I doubt that you and your superior would be, either. That may be why you set your cunning trap for us: to make sure you would never have to face us yourselves."

Current laughed. "Close enough, Amazon! Onion's right; you would make a fine mistress, properly declawed and defanged. But know this: Purp, as you call him, could easily have killed all of you had he wanted to. But while he earned the rank as leader, he was rash, vain, and inexperienced in all aspects of leadership, and nearly brought the conquest to disaster. He was really more focused on showing off his power and abilities than on killing enemies like you, which was one of his biggest flaws. My superior and I will not make the same mistake." He paused, then added, "With one exception."

"If you think to spare my life so that you can use me as a mistress," Helena said evenly, "that mistake could cost you your life. Don't gamble on it."

"Aptly spoken," Current said. "Much as I admire your poise and defiance under pressure, and appreciate the splendor of your body, I have no intention of sparing you. You are absolutely correct."

"Benny!" Helena said, putting elements together. "He's the one. That's why Onion is afraid of him."

Onion, standing beside Current, winced.

"Why?" Benny demanded. "I have no connection to you."

"Ah, but that is where you are wrong, my naive associate. How is your mother?"

Benny was so surprised he spluttered. "My mother! What does she have to do with it?"

"Everything."

"Well, she's never been part of my life. She deserted me as a baby, and I think she's long dead. Even if she lives, she has no interest in me, nor I in her."

"You are mistaken."

Despite his perilous circumstance, Benny was annoyed. "What the hell do you know about it?"

"One more question, then I will answer. What is her name?"

"Winona. That's just about the sum total of what I know about her. Winona Witch."

"Correct. She is also a vampire."

Benny's jaw dropped. Current seemed to know. But how could that be? "I—" But he was unable to finish.

"This is perhaps, why you were attracted to a vampire. There is that blood in you, though it never manifested openly."

"You—you know about Virtue?"

"I call her Laurel. She was mine before she was yours."

Preposterous! "But she was a virgin!"

Current smiled. "Hardly. But she seemed that way to you, and, of course, she did not advertise that aspect of her past. But this is a detail, rather than the main theme, which explains my interest in you."

"Main theme?"

Current frowned. "Now listen, innocent man, because your welfare depends on it. Winona had three sons by three different men. The second was Aiken, who never amounted to much. The third, by a human man, was you."

Benny was reluctantly fascinated, and he knew his companions were, too, despite their dire situation. "Who was the first?"

"Her first son was by a blue demon. That son was me."

Was the man trying to tease him? Yet, there was a blue cast about him, apart from his clothing. "I have trouble believing that."

"Winona lives today. She has directed me to recruit you. She wants you on our side."

"Recruit me! Never!"

"We know you are opposed, but there are inducements," Current said. "Agree, and your companions will be spared torture and death."

"Don't sell out for us!" Dale said, and Helena nodded.

"And you will be reunited with Mother, who does love you, in her fashion. She is proud of your career to date."

Benny was revolted, but could not be sure the man was lying. "What of Virtue?"

"Ah, you drive a hard bargain. You may have her, too, if you want her."

"*If* I want her? I love her!"

"She is mine now. I rape her at will. She is a fallen woman. I may kill her rather than let her go, after I demean her some more. But if this is the price of you, and you still want her, I will pay it. I'm sure she'd be happier with you, though she does retain feeling for me."

Benny had had enough. If he still wanted his abused beloved? Who might have some feeling for her abuser? This man was trying to play him, and he did not know if anything Onion said could be believed. So he called the bluff. "No! Go to hell!"

Current nodded, unperturbed. "I will tell Mother I tried, but you were unreasonable." He turned to Onion. "Our paymaster will reward you handsomely for your service, and I add my appreciation. Now the prisoners are yours to do with whatever you wish, with one restriction: do not kill or seriously damage Benny Clout. You may make him hurt, but he must survive intact, in case he should change his mind at a later date. I do not want Mother unduly wroth with me." Then, he got up and walked away.

"Good enough," Onion said, well satisfied. He looked at Helena. "Such a tempting figure! But if Ammarod is cautious about toying with you, I think I'd better not risk it, even keeping you thoroughly trussed up. But there are other ways to have at an Amazon."

The Kudgels staked the four firmly to the ground. Then, Onion wrapped a small hank of Helena's hair around a rod and pulled on it until it was ripped out of her head, along with some of her scalp, leaving a bleeding wound. She made no sound.

"This has been merely a token demonstration; be assured there is worse coming in due course." He paused. "Or maybe you'd prefer to indulge my passion?" he inquired with a leer. "I may spare your lovely hair if you give your word not to fight back in any manner."

Benny found it interesting that the elf would take her given word in a situation like this. He knew an Amazon would not violate her oath.

Now, she spoke. "Never!" And there was the proof of it: she refused to give her word, which she would not break even to escape him.

"We'll see. Once you die, you should be safe to plumb for a few hours before we give your corpse to the dragons. So, I will have you, my dear, alive or dead, your choice."

He moved on to Dale. "I suspect you value your hands. We'll start with the fingers."

Dale did not react as a Kudgel took hold of the littlest finger on his left hand and hammered a tack under the nail. It had to hurt horrendously, but it was as if Dale were asleep. "And there is your token, big man," Onion said. "We'll do the others and the toes, in due course. Then we'll start in more seriously. I look forward to it."

The elf moved on to Burgundy. "I hear this guy is into horny dreams. Let's give him something to dream about."

The Kudgels heaved the dwarf onto a raised framework, naked, facedown. Then, they hung a weight to his genital that slowly stretched it down toward the ground. It was obviously painful, but, like the others, Burgundy made no sound.

"When it touches the ground, we'll hack it off," Onion said. "I mean the flesh, not the weight. So enjoy your hour of stretching; have a good sleep and dream."

Then, he moved on to Benny. "I'll take that hat. That's Jack's hat, that he stole from me years ago." He snatched it and put it on his own head. "Can't hurt you too badly," he said, considering. "Especially since you might change your mind about joining the Kudgels. Fortunately, we do have time." He brightened. "I know: flaying, a little at a time."

He brought out a tiny knife and used it as a scalpel, slicing an oblong pattern into Benny's left forearm. Then, he put a small hook in one end and slowly pulled the skin away from the muscle beneath. It hurt horrendously, but Benny gritted his teeth and did not cry out. The strip came loose, leaving the pattern on the arm to well blood.

"Can't have you bleed too much; it's messy," Onion said. "So we'll salt it." He slapped a sponge soaked in salt water on the wound. That hurt worse, as it was supposed to; it was all Benny could do to keep himself from screaming. He was sustained mainly by rage: that this pipsqueak, imitation warrior had such power to hurt them just for the dubious fun of it. Oh, Onion did want some things, such as to safely have sex with Helena, or to get Benny to change sides. But mainly, he was just indulging his propensity for hurting others. He was the one who deserved to be tortured to death.

Onion glanced at the sky. "Dinner time. We'll let you be for now, and return when we are suitably fortified. You folk are not hungry, of course." There was no reaction to his continued baiting. That did not seem to slow him. "Oh, I almost forget. We don't want you trying anything while we relax. So we'll give you a little drink to make you nod off for an hour or so." He snapped his fingers, and the Kudgels brought out small cups filled with thick liquid. They held the captives' mouths open and poured it down their throats, not caring if they choked. It was easier simply to swallow it. It did not taste bad, actually, but Benny deeply distrusted it. A pleasant numbness was spreading from his stomach; where would it stop?

The Kudgels walked away, going to their mess tent. Onion hung back a moment. "Pleasant dreams, folks," he said, then followed, his stolen hat perched jauntily.

They were alone again, for the hour. That, of course, was also suspicious. What were the Kudgels up to now?

"I know this potion," Helena said. "It doesn't just put you to sleep, it wipes your memory, for a time. It's used as a truth serum, and as an aid to rape."

"It does, and is," Dale agreed. "It will make us forget recent events. Forget our scruples. This may be another ploy to get you to loosen your legs, Helena, as you won't remember why not and won't much care. And to make you change sides, Benny, as you won't remember which side you're on."

"Damn!" Burgundy swore. "You mean I won't even remember the women I've had, after I lose my member?" Because it had stretched almost to the ground.

"For a while," Helena said. "But you'll remember again after a few days, if you live."

"Benny," Dale said urgently. "This stuff is taking hold. We're doomed when it does. Don't you think it's time to do your trick? Before you forget how?"

Somehow, Benny had not thought of his ghosting ability, which usually manifested only in moments of dire stress. Well, this was that! He stepped out of his bonds, then went to Dale and ripped out the stakes that anchored his ropes to the ground. Then, Dale went to do the same for Helena, while Benny freed Burgundy.

But already the elixir was making him dizzy. "Get out of here!" he cried. "Anywhere! Just get away and hide before they come after us."

"We'll have an hour or less," Dale said. "They'll catch us for sure."

"The hell they will," Helena said grimly as she went to recover her weapons from the pile of netting. Then, she charged the Kudgels' mess tent.

Good strategy. The four of them, kept alert by rage, got their weapons and fell on the hapless Kudgels and slaughtered them. Benny especially wanted to get Onion, but he was not there. Evidently, he had gone instead to an officer's mess tent. "Damn!" Benny gritted, hacking at tent poles and canvas, anything that was there.

"Take it easy," Dale cautioned. "We'll be asleep soon regardless, and these aren't the only Kudgels. Flee before others come."

He was making sense.

"In different directions," Helena said. "So they can't catch all of us. We can get together again later."

She was making sense too.

They split up, running in four directions. Already, there was the sound of other Kudgels who were just starting to catch on that there was trouble afoot.

*****

Now, Benny faced Onion, infuriated. He was halfway drunk, but his rage was burning back the fog. He focused on just one thing: killing the arrogant elf.

"Benny the Buffoon," the elf sneered. "Who needs a spanking."

Caution. It was the voice of the Protector. But Benny was beyond caution. He knew better than to draw his sword here in a tavern, where such an act would violate the code. He picked up a glass bottle of rum and smashed it against a table, breaking off the main part. He charged the elf and sliced open his neck, quickly and messily killing him.

Now, Onion's men charged him, their weapons drawn. The code was hopelessly compromised, and Benny was guilty; they could kill him with impunity. The Protector's warning had been relevant.

But Benny had his magic staff. The Kudgels were unfamiliar with it, and did not guard properly against it. In moments, all of them were dead.

Now, he was able to calm himself. "Sorry about that," he told the astonished bartender. "There were old scores to settle."

"You're a beast!" the man said. "Leave my premises!"

"Gladly." It meant the man was afraid of him and didn't want to tangle with him. It was best to avoid further trouble.

"But first, tell me who you are."

Onion had called him Benny the Buffoon. The bartender had called him a beast. Both were true, to an extent. The two came neatly together. "Benny the Beast. And don't forget it."

Then, his drunken stupor returning, Benny left the premises and continued on up the road. Now, the things he had learned from his flashback returned to cause him grief. It wasn't just that Onion had tortured all the members of the party; the elf had paid for that with his miserable life. It wasn't just that the party had become hopelessly separated, and Benny didn't know the fate of the others. Or his own fate, for that matter, as he remained lost.

It was what Ammarod Current had told him of Virtue and himself. He didn't want to believe any of it, but the man had no reason to lie. How he had brutalized and raped Virtue, whom he had known before Benny did. For that, Current had to die.

Yet there was the other. That Current was Benny's half-brother. That they had the same mother, Winona, who was not only alive, but on the other side. That she was part vampire, which meant that Benny was part vampire too. He had known she was a witch; what else had she passed along to him? Did his ghosting power stem from that? And she wanted Benny to join them. That was anathema!

But if he agreed, he could save Virtue.

That was the sticking point. He would do anything for Virtue. But he would never betray his own side. He had to kill Current. But that would sacrifice Virtue, for she was surely hostage to Current's life. And how could he kill his brother? He was stuck between irresistible alternatives. He had to decide—and could not.

He wrestled with that as he walked.

Until he passed out on the street.

Chapter 8
Coming Together

Helena considered the map. It seemed to cover everything but one thing: where were the other members of the party? They had scattered in four directions so as to be difficult to recapture, but this also made it difficult for them to reunite. What good was it knowing where things were if she didn't know where *they* were?

Well, she knew that Dale would have the holy dwarf city of Alfen Gulfadex in mind, and well might head for it. That was where she was most likely to find him. Then they could see about finding the others.

Unfortunately, now that she had decided, she discovered an obscurity in the map. The city was marked on it, but the route through the mountains was fuzzed out. It seemed that something did not want the route to be known, and the map reflected that. She would have to pick her own way through, and that could be mischief.

What would be would be. She paused to organize her facilities for a possibly dangerous trek. And felt something.

It was...it was the soft ambiance of someone she knew rather intimately. Green and purple, no, magenta. Magenta! The late Purp's sister, now to be the leader of the Kudgels, if she could just get them to obey her. A lovely, fine, compassionate person. Helena had lent her body for Magenta to animate when bidding farewell to her brother as he lay dying; that was why she knew the feel of the woman. She had, in effect, become Magenta for the occasion, and it had left an imprint on her soul. She believed in her, and trusted her. In an obscure but profound way, she loved Magenta.

If Magenta needed to borrow her body again, for some local purpose, she was welcome to it. Helena relaxed, letting the spirit take her.

And found herself transported not to another person, but another place. She recognized it: Dale's mansion in Upper Sultry. Which was far away. Was she imagining it?

Magenta was there, standing before her, her skin and eyes green, face hair, hands and feet purple, and utterly lovely. "Thank you for allowing me to bring you here, Helena," Magenta said. "May I embrace you?"

Helena had to smile. "You have been closer to me than that."

The woman hugged her. "I feel that I know you well, though our contacts have been peripheral. You are a good woman."

"So are you. But how did you move me here?"

"I am still learning to use the magics I inherited from my brother. Among them is a teleportation stone. I had to reach you telepathically, which I could do when I tried, because there is now some of each of us in the other. We have, in a manner, become sisters. Then, I needed your acquiescence. When you granted that, I was able to draw on the power of the stone to bring you to me physically. Now, we can catch up on details and work together toward the common mission of saving our world."

"I was looking for Dale," Helena said. "This is his house."

"Yes. He is bound to return here at some point."

"We have to stop the Kudgels from blowing the horn that summons the Sky Titans, lest they destroy everything."

"Yes, of course. But we need also to stop the Kudgels from laying waste that 'everything.' Most of all, we need to coordinate our efforts so we do not work at cross purposes. Meanwhile, we can relax and catch up on things, as I will not be able to use the stone again for several hours; I'm not sure whether it is I or the stone that needs to recover between efforts."

Helena knew that the energy of teleportation could not have come from nowhere. It was probably a joint contribution, depleting both woman and stone, at least for a while. "We can relax," she agreed.

"Tell me what you have been doing recently. I made mental contact with you, but I didn't read your mind; I merely verified your identity and location."

Helena launched into the story of their travel, capture, torture, and escape. "And so I learned of Dale's father," she concluded. "And his little half-sister, Noletta, a fine girl who can do illusions. She actually saved my life by scaring away the pursuing Kudgels." She smiled. "And her mother, the dryad Desdemona, who inhabited a white ash tree, and I think has not entirely left them despite her death." She lifted the pendant. "I must deliver this to Dale, so that he knows. Or rather, its twin, so we each have one. If he accepts it, there will be a rapprochement with his father."

"May I touch it?" Magenta asked.

Helena held out the pendant, still on its chain around her neck. Magenta touched it. There was a thrill of mutual recognition. The woman and the dryad liked each other.

"And your story," Helena said. "What have you been doing since we last interacted?"

"I have been struggling to learn my proper role, and the powers I have come to possess. Since my brother's death, the Kudgel factions have split. Half are surrendering and seeking peace, following my guidance because I am Purp's sister. The other half remain true to the original Kudgel war, following Ammarod Current and another leader whose identity I do not yet know. It is roughly in balance at the moment, but the tide will shift, and either I will prevail or Ammarod will."

"Ammarod," Helena said. "I know little of him."

"He is a monster!"

"Surely so. But I am also mystified by how your brother, Purp, got around so widely so as to be active in seemingly many places at once."

"That I can tell you," Magenta said. "He used the stones I am now learning. I can't yet do it as well as he did, but I am slowly gaining proficiency. There are a number of them stashed at key locations. They enabled him to see their areas, and then to travel to them telepathically. That was how I brought you here: first I saw you, then I fetched you. But this Ammarod—he is a demon, or at least part demon. He can dematerialize and jump to distant places without needing the stones. That makes him doubly dangerous. He's absolutely horrible."

"So you said," Helena said. "But what makes him worse than Purp?"

"I am not sure I should tell you. It's ugly."

"I can handle it, and I think I need to know. What is it?"

"I was experimenting with the several stones, orienting on one and then another, not yet trying to teleport there, just feeling out the terrain. And Ammarod was there at one and sensed me. He recognized me, maybe because he knew my brother, so was attuned. His mind was sheer malignancy."

Helena saw the scene as Magenta narrated it. The two minds were hovering near the stone, forming into ghostly figures. One was the lovely woman, the other a handsome man. But appearance was superficial; their personalities were quite different.

"Give it up, purple flower," Ammarod thought to her. "You can't win, and might as well make it easier on yourself."

"Who are you?" she replied, startled by being thus recognized when it was only a trace of her mind there.

"I am Ammarod, new leader of the Kudgels, and this world will be mine."

"You are not," Magenta responded, annoyed. "I am the leader. They follow me."

"*Half* of them follow you, you delicious creature. The rest follow me. All will follow me once I dispose of you."

"What makes you suppose you can win their loyalty from me?"

"I am powerful and competent in ways your stupid brother was not. I take what I want and destroy the rest. You must either join me or suffer rape and death, as your friend Virtue Vampire is suffering now."

"Virtue!" she exclaimed, shocked by the reference. "She is not a combatant."

"She is merely a victim. I beat her up and raped her, and will kill her when I am done with her. That will be when I have another pretty doll to take my fancy." He stared lewdly at her. "And I believe that will be you, with the added convenience of bringing your followers back to the true cause. So you're next, you colorful creature."

Appalled by his threat, Magenta vacated the site and jumped her mind to observe Virtue. One look satisfied her that it was true: the lovely vampire had been brutalized. He really did do such things to women. And now she knew that the demon was tracking her.

"That is why I came here to Dale's mansion," Magenta concluded. "It has wards against magical intrusion, and magic of its own. I am safe here. Meanwhile, I continue to organize. Ammarod must be stopped."

"Ammarod must be stopped," Helena agreed, similarly appalled. "Poor Benny! Does he know?"

"I don't think so, and I don't know how I will tell him. This is already awful."

"It is," Helena agreed. "I must rejoin the others and stop the Kudgels from blowing that horn."

"I must help you in that, and continue organizing my Kudgels. I hope to establish peaceful relations between my good Kudgels and Upper Sultry. Here, let me give you this." She fetched a small tubular object.

"What is this?"

"It is a special flute that will alert me ahead of time when to teleport to Alfen Gulfadex, to join your group there. Make sure to play it ahead of time, as it will take me a while to set up the teleportation."

"I will," Helena said, moved.

"Now, I will send you back to where you were so you can resume your search for the others. I will search too; if they pass near one of the stones, I may see them."

"May all of us be lucky," Helena said fervently.

They kissed each other in parting.

Then, Helena was back where she had been, traveling north, but now with greater confidence.

Dale and Burgundy resumed their trek north, but now they had a map that would guide them through the perilous passes of the mountains. That made all the difference.

Then, there came an awareness to Dale's mind. There was a presence he remembered, with a green and purple association. "Magenta!" he exclaimed.

"What?" the dwarf asked, startled.

"I felt her nearness. Her mind, at least."

"What does she want?"

"I'm not sure." He focused on the feeling, accepting it.

Then the two of them were in his mansion. There was Magenta standing before them. "It worked!" she said, pleased.

"What worked?" he asked, confused.

"I came here because your house is safe," she said. "Helena was here, looking for you. I said I would look, too, and I did, but I did not expect to find you so soon. I had no idea you'd be so near the sage's scrolls. So I used the teleportation stone to bring you both in. I found more than one stone, so I can do it without having to recuperate as long." She went on to explain about the stones, to their amazement.

"We just visited the sages," Dale explained. "They granted us safe passage through the mountains to Alfen Gulfadex. We have a map."

"Then you should be able to catch up with Helena on the trail. I was trying to teleport you there so you could connect more rapidly. Had I known I would find you so quickly I would have kept her here. But you will surely find her soon on your own."

"Yes, we should," Dale agreed enthusiastically.

Burgundy was silent. "Are you all right?" Magenta inquired solicitously.

"Forgive me," the dwarf said.

"Forgive you what? I don't believe we have met before."

"That's it. I thought we would never meet. I dreamed of you."

"Dreamed of me?"

"When I sleep I have passionate relations with beautiful women. You were delightful. But now that I see you in person I fear you will be annoyed."

"So you were the dwarf I sensed last night," Magenta said. "Passionate is an understatement."

Burgundy hung his head. "Yes, ma'am."

She laughed. "Be at ease, lover. For years, I was a prostitute. I had relations with hundreds of men. Some were giants, some were dwarves like yourself. Some had truly weird urges. You were in the middle range. Certainly better than what I face if we lose this war."

"What you face?"

"Ammarod Current desires me. I don't desire him. He is an evil demon. I would much rather be with you."

The dwarf was amazed and gratified. Dale suspected that, while what Magenta said might be true, that did not necessarily indicate that she liked Burgundy, merely that he was less worse than the demon. But he kept his mouth shut. The woman was being kind.

Then, she conjured them back to where they had been. Now they had far more confidence.

✦

Benny woke on a pallet in a dark tent, by a small fire, clutching his staff. He knew he must have spent several hours passed out drunk in the street, and must have had an awful hangover, but actually he felt reasonably well. Someone must have dosed him with an antidote. Why? That bothered him almost as much as the hangover would have. He had provoked more fighting than he needed to, and killed a number of people who probably didn't deserve it. Onion, he didn't regret, but the others were only peripheral and could have been spared with a warning beating. He was not proud of himself.

The tent flap opened and a figure entered. It was a woman with milk white skin, black eyes, blue lips, and razor teeth. There were black lines on her face in the shape of a pentagram. Her hair was glossy black, hanging thickly to her knees; the hanks looked almost prehensile, though that might have been from the flickering light of the fire. Her torso was lithe and shapely; though she was clearly not young, there was a sensual appeal to her that manifested with every movement of her limbs and hips. She wore a tight blouse and pants that seemed almost to be formed of moss, as if it were growing on her skin. It shifted color as she moved, now brown, now green, now with a touch of iridescence. Also, gloves and slippers of the same material, if material it was, with only her fingernails and toenails glistening beyond. Overall, the effect was naughtily fascinating, surely by no accident. There was a musky odor to her, not exactly perfume, but hellishly erotic. She was a seductress, and likely a witch.

She squatted before him, and the sex appeal of her supple thighs was palpable. She smiled, and to his surprise her features softened into undertones of kindness and even goodness; now, her blue lips seemed friendly rather than alien. The contrast with the rest of her aspect was startling;

it was as though good and evil were woven through her in the manner of an exotic carpet, each somehow enhancing the other. Benny knew immediately that she meant him no ill. In fact, she must have been the one who fetched him here and treated him to abate the bruises and headache he had earned the day before. "Benny," she murmured, and her voice was a somber caress.

"That's me," he agreed, stroked by that voice. "Who are you, and what am I doing here?"

"You are recovering from an overindulgence," she said. "I found you unconscious, clutching your staff. I could not remove it from your hand; the wood resisted me with magical force." She shook her hand reminiscently. "I thought it was a mere walking aid, but it is a weapon."

"I won it from the Emperor of Upper Sultry, as a prize. It's a potent implement that responds only to me."

"Ah, yes, the Emperor. We do not get along." She reached forth and stroked his forehead, and her touch made his skin tingle pleasantly. "Fear not; all will be well."

"Why are you helping me? I don't think I know you."

She laughed. "You have been in me, and you don't know me?"

"I never had intimate relations with you!" Benny glared. "I would remember if I had." Unless, he thought, that mind-deadening elixir had wiped it out. The prospect of sex with her both repelled and fascinated him. She was too old and too witchy, but still sexy as only a succubus could be.

"It was some time ago, dearest Benny. About a quarter century."

"A quarter century! I was a baby then!"

Then he froze, staring at her. Was it possible? Not sex, but birth?

"Yes," she said as if reading his mind. "I am Winona."

His mother! He realized that her age was right. That would explain why she was helping him.

"Mother," he breathed, reluctantly coming to believe. "But—"

"It is true, my son. It is from me you got your inner magic." She smiled. "And your taste for vampires, which Ammarod shares. Because of that part of my ancestry."

His ghosting ability, that had saved his life more than once. And his love of Virtue? He feared it was true. "But I hate Ammarod," he said. "He brutalized and raped my beloved wife. I will one day kill him for that."

"I wanted better things for you, my son, than witchery," she said. "That is why I left you in good human hands, with your father, though it hurt me to lose you and your father. I kept your brother Aiken too long, and he turned out useless. It was worse with Ammarod; he became a warlock and a warrior, but with a core of viciousness I could not expunge. Yet I must work with him, though he is a bad man. He is, after all, my son, and the son of the blue demon I love." She touched her blue lips reminiscently. "The demon gave me these. They say that witches can't love, but I have loved twice, in addition to my children. I loved the demon first, but wrenched myself away from him to preserve my sanity and went to your father. Then, when I joined the Kudgels, the demon came back into my life, and I reconciled with him. Sanity is overrated."

Benny's mind was spinning. He grasped a sliver. "Ammarod. He said he worked with his superior to take over the Kudgel army."

"Yes, I am that superior," Winona said. "I do retain ultimate power over him, so far."

"So far?"

"Ammarod is gaining power, and he lacks sensible restrictions. He will inevitably turn against me in time, and his father won't stop him. I have just one hope: your core of goodness, Benny, is huge compared to mine. Join us, and we can govern the Kudgels effectively. That is why I intervened to spare you. Together, we can make the Kudgel Empire mighty, without suffering the mayhem that will occur if

Ammarod takes over. By so doing, you will also be able to spare your wife further mischief. You can save her, Benny."

Benny realized that there was a rationale. But to join her would be to cast aside his lifelong belief in doing what was right. He would inevitably be corrupted, and that was a greater evil than what he had encountered so far. "No."

Winona sighed. "I had hoped to persuade you by the logic of my case, and by the inducements I offered, such as enormous power and the life of your vampire wife. But I see I must instead use magic." She raised her dark hands.

"No!" he repeated, and swept his staff around to block her. "Don't make me hurt you, Mother!"

"Oh, I doubt you have the power to do that physically." Her hands began to glow. "Emotionally, yes; it does hurt to be rejected by one's child. But that will surely change." The glow intensified.

This was mischief. He had to stop her before she overpowered him with her magic. Benny swung the staff at her, hard, hoping that its power would cancel hers, leaving only its physical force as if it were an ordinary staff. It could knock her back, hurt her physically, or at least enable him to escape her.

He saw the surprise in her face as she realized that this was true. He was balking her.

Then she and the tent vanished. Or rather, maybe it was Benny who vanished.

He found himself at Dale's Mansion.

"Benny Clout!" Magenta exclaimed. "I found you just in time and teleported you to safety. That witch was about to enchant you."

Benny glanced at his staff, deciding not to argue that case. Certainly she had rescued him from an ugly situation. "Thank you." He had encountered Magenta before only in telepathic animation; now she was physically present, and even lovelier.

"Your group needs to be united to stop the Kudgels," she said. Then, she hesitated. "There is something you need to know about Virtue. It's not good. I don't know how to tell you."

"That Ammarod is raping her," Benny said with cold fury. "You know!"

"He told me. He's proud of it. I need to kill him."

"Oh, Benny, I'm so sorry! We have to save her. But Ammarod has awful power. He threatens to do the same to me, when he gets the chance. I'm afraid of him."

"I know. He's half blue demon. And my half-brother."

She stared at him. "This is worse yet."

"I have to kill my brother," Benny said, voicing his terrible dilemma. "To save my beloved."

"Yes, I fear it is so. I am so sorry, Benny."

Then, somehow they were sitting on the bed in the room Benny had shared with Virtue when they were here at the Mansion, and Magenta had her arms about him, comforting him. She was warm and soft and wonderful. "Oh, dammit!" he swore tearfully into her warm green shoulder.

"Exactly," she agreed.

"What am I doing here with you, when I should be with Virtue?"

"I don't know," she said. "Yet, somehow it seems right."

That was the thing: it did seem right. Magenta was not trying to seduce him or confuse him, only to help him. How could this be? It was as if they had a relationship, if not in the past or the present, maybe in the future.

"I—I want to kiss you," he said. "Feel free to slap my face."

"Benny, you know my past. If it helps you to kiss me, then do it. If it helps you to sleep with me, then do it. I am anybody's girl."

"You're the leader of half the Kudgels!"

"That, too," she agreed with a wan smile. "But right now, with you, I am just a friend."

Benny realized it was true. Their paths had crossed peripherally so far, but they were on the same side and he trusted her. "I shouldn't be taking your time."

"You are important, too, Benny. As I sense the flows of this dreadful war, I know that you are integral to its outcome. You are as important as I am, and I must help you to accomplish your portion of it. So if kissing me as an anonymous woman enables that, do it. It is personally meaningless."

"No. I want to kiss you as if it means something."

"Don't do that!" she said, alarmed. "It is emotionally meaningful only with Virtue."

"Who has been despoiled."

"Benny, it wasn't her choice! She needs you now more than ever."

"Yes! I wish I could be with her, at least to reassure her that I still love her."

"I wish I could conjure her here for you. But there's no stone close enough. Neither can I conjure you to her, only to where I found you."

Then Benny thought of something. "Magenta, when you had to visit your brother Purp, before he died—"

"That was different. We had the help of an established vampire telepath, and a local host, Helena, who lent me her body. I visited him in simulation."

"Yes. And I saw Helena, who is not at all like you in appearance or manner, become you. It was amazing. It was just as if you were personally there."

"I *was* there, but only in simulation. An extended illusion enabled by our mental rapport." She smiled. "It left us both close friends, for such a merger never completely fades. The Amazon is a fine woman."

"That is my point. Magenta, could you do the same with Virtue?"

She shook her head. "There would be no point in using her as a host to animate me at her home. She needs to be with you, not me."

"The other way around. Could she animate you, here?"

Her mouth fell open. "Oh, my! If I could reach her mind, yes, I could bring her to me in that manner."

"Please, Magenta! I know it's a lot to ask of you, but it would mean so much to us both."

She considered briefly, and decided. "That must be why you want to kiss me. You want to kiss *her*—in my body."

"Yes. I can appreciate how you wouldn't want to do it."

"I do want to do it! But first I must locate her more solidly, not just to glance in passing, and commune with her, to be sure it is right with her. You must relax, while I range outward. I know where she lives; what I need to find is a stone close enough to enable this partial alignment."

"Thank you."

For the rest of the day, Benny relaxed, ate, snoozed, and explored the premises, while Magenta sat and looked like a zombie, her mind ranging.

Then, in the early evening, she came to life. "I found a stone!" she exclaimed. "It's an old one, not sufficient for teleportation, but it will do nicely for sustained mental rapport."

"Wonderful!"

"Let me prepare." She gobbled down some food, took a quick shower, toweled herself dry while he watched, bemused, then changed into a filmy nightshift that hardly concealed her attractive feminine form.

"What are you doing?" Benny asked, embarrassed that he found that form so appealing. "I thought you were going to—"

Then her aspect shifted. Her colors faded, and her purple hair became fair, reaching to her knees. "Benny," she breathed as gentle fangs showed.

It was Virtue.

He ran to her and enfolded her. "Virtue!"

She held back only a moment. "I have been despoiled by another man. I will understand if you turn away."

115

"Never!" he kissed her, and it was Virtue's kiss. He bore her to the bed, and in moments they were making desperate love.

"Oh, Benny," she said as they lay beside each other. "How I have longed for this moment."

"I love you! I never want to leave you."

"Yet you face hard choices."

"Awful choices," he agreed. "But when I think of what Ammarod is doing to you I get so angry I can't think straight. Will you forgive me if I kill him?"

"This is difficult. I know he is evil, but he was my lover before I knew you, and I do retain some feeling for him. You are the one I want to be with, Benny, but I don't want to have him killed, much as I know he deserves it."

"And there is the dilemma."

They ceased talking and made love again. Then they slept, holding hands.

They woke several times in the night, their fervor flaring like a flickering fire. They simply couldn't get enough of each other. They had never been this passionate in their regular life, but, of course, this was special.

Virtue was still there in the morning. "I am sorry, but I must leave you now," she said. "Magenta has been wonderful, but she is tiring, and the magic of the stone is depleted."

"Oh, Virtue!" He held her and kissed her, trying to postpone the leaving, but her body changed and he found himself holding and kissing Magenta. "Oops!" He quickly disengaged.

"I'm so sorry," Magenta said. "I am exhausted." Then, she dropped off to sleep, literally: her lifted head plopped to the pillow.

Benny got out of bed and dressed, leaving her there. It had of course been her body throughout, and her awareness within it, observing while he embraced Virtue. She had done a marvelously self-sacrificing thing. She was beautiful in her own right, inside and outside, and she had done him a matchless favor.

After a few hours, Magenta woke and got up, cleaned up, and changed clothing. "I apologize for leaving you on your own," she said.

"Magenta, what you did for me was phenomenal. You gave me back my beloved for a few hours. I regret only that your generous self-sacrifice wore you out for nothing."

She made a gesture of dismissal. "It was not for nothing, Benny. You are a fine man, the kind I would wish to have for myself. I liked being in your embrace, even if anonymously. Now I must return you to the place where I found you so you can resume your mission, and I can resume mine."

She liked him personally? Benny realized that he also liked her personally. She was an amazing woman. But he did not feel free to say that, considering the rather mixed nature of their association. "I'll need to find the others, if they survive."

"They do survive," she said. "Helena is at Scroll Castle, which is not far north of the witch's tent. Winona set it there near the village to intercept you."

"Thank you," he said. "For everything."

"You are welcome—to everything."

Magenta stood before him, oriented on the distant magic stone, and suddenly, Benny found himself back at Winona's tent. The witch was not there, fortunately. He quickly departed.

Soon, he found the castle of the sages. Helena was there, evidently expecting him. "Magenta sent me a mental message," she explained. "We now have a certain telepathic rapport."

"Great! You are all right? I see your hair is growing back."

She touched the place where the lock of hair was gone. "Yes." Then she turned serious. "Benny, I have bad news. I met with the survivors. The sages—it seems that the men went out to do battle with Ammarod and his Kudgels. They were prepared for that. But they were ambushed by the witch."

"Winona!"

"Yes, that is what they call her. She has powers the sages did not reckon with, and quickly captured them so that Ammarod could consume their life essences. He has the ability to increase his life and power by absorbing that of his victims. The sage men are gone. Only the women and children remain, as they were protected within Scroll Castle. It will be a generation before their community is fully functional again."

"This is terrible!"

"It is," she agreed. "The only good thing is that their servant woman, Trista, told me where the safe passage into the Northern Mountains is, and that Dale and Burgundy are there. We must go there now."

"Yes," he agreed numbly. He had not known the sages personally, but had understood that they were allies. They had paid an awful price!

They hiked north, catching each other up on their separate adventures, and in due course, reached the pass. There were Dale and the dwarf. Helena hugged Dale while Benny saluted Burgundy.

"Dale, I have something for you," Helena said, lifting the second white ash chip. "Don't argue, just take it." She put the chain over his neck. He looked surprised, but let it stay.

Their group was reunited at last. Now all they had to do was stop the Kudgels from blowing the Gold Horn to summon the Sky Titans.

Chapter 9
Alfen Gulfadex

For several days, the companions ascended the Northern Mountains. Benny had thought the Gant Mountains enormous in his youth, but they seemed mere anthills compared to those he now traversed. He and the others quickly realized that, without proper knowledge of this footpath, it would be all but impossible to reach Alfen Gulfadex. The entire journey, they walked single file along the path, the mountain ascending at an impossibly steep angle into the clouds, and descending at the same deadly angle on the other side. While it curved gradually with the contour of the mountains, the pathway was surprisingly clear of debris, and the gigantic cedars of the forest of the mountains provided shade, as well as a natural barrier to the deadly slope descending the mountain side. While they stopped for short periods of rest to relieve themselves or consume what edibles they had or could find, they did not sleep; that could be done once they reached Alfen Gulfadex. To pass the time, they shared the stories of their journeys. Soon, along with Benny's rejuvenated memory, they all remembered the details of their separation, and were amazed at what had transpired.

"I thought Helena here was a freaky fantasy, but Winona Witch sounds simply irresistible," Burgundy raised his hands when Benny shot him a glance, "No offense, Ben. I know it's probably not very pleasant…hearing me rant about your mom like that."

"Don't call her that. She may have given birth to me, but she will never be my mother. She abandoned my father, Aiken, and I before I was even old enough to remember. That's bad enough, but even that doesn't compare to how she's allowed herself to become twisted...demonic. She's given herself to demons and black magic. She's probably killed countless innocents in her allegiance to the Kudgels; she's manipulated Ammarod, and tried to turn me against you, Pakk, and everything I stand for. She and Ammarod can both go to hell!" Benny violently kicked a pebble on the ground.

Dale shook his head. "Don't say that, Benny. Hate their actions and beliefs, but don't hate them. Everything starts out good...I did, you did, and I'm sure your mother and Ammarod were once good souls. But life can turn even the greatest of saints into devils. We don't know their stories, and it doesn't excuse their actions, just as your drunkenness and thirst for vengeance doesn't excuse your killing of Belasco and his gang, nor do my emotions excuse me my ill deeds."

"Well, what the hell am I supposed to feel? Friends have been killed, cities and countries have been devastated and overwhelmed, and the very existence of Pakk is at stake because of them, and people like them!"

"Dale's right," Helena said, "You have a right to be upset...even to use lethal force on your mother and brother in order to stop them, but that shouldn't be our goal."

"And what's that, Helena? To bend over and take it up the ass?!" Benny shouted, his voice echoing through the trees.

"Might wanna hold your tongue, Ben. That kinda talk gets me excited!" Benny couldn't help but chuckle at Burgundy's remark.

"Our goal should be to stop them, not kill them," Dale said. "To help bring about the best outcome for everyone. Do you forget the mercy you and dear Virtue had on me?

I was as bad, if not worse, than your mother and Ammarod have ever been. If anyone deserved to die for their evildoing, it was me. But you saw through my evil, to the goodness I had locked away inside myself. I'm not saying it's easy, or even possible, for you to change your mother and brother's ways...to make them see the light. Some, unfortunately, are beyond that. But we should still hope for the best. If you allow your vengeance and hatred of your family to consume you...yes, family is exactly what they are...you'll be no better than them and perhaps worse for it. Understand what I'm saying, Benny the Beast?" Dale looked over his shoulder at Benny, and he shuddered with shame at the look of disappointment on his mentor's disfigured face.

"I can't just let it go, Dale...especially not after what Ammarod did to my Virtue!"

"I'm not saying to forget what they did, or to not hold them accountable. I'm saying that you have to forgive them. Let go of the hatred, the anger. That's what I should've done, long ago, but I held it in, and soon it was beyond my power to change. It took Virtue to do that. Do you want the life I had? Do you want the memory of murdering, raping, and ruining the lives of countless men, women, and children, of all races of beings? I doubt it, sincerely."

"I hear what you're saying...still..." Benny's face was red with rage.

"Good God, boy, what would Jack think if he saw you like this?" Dale retorted.

Benny was struck to the core. The memory of Jack didn't take away the hate he felt for his kin, or the Kudgels. However, he realized he had to at least try to do what Dale was suggesting. But there was an anger inside him that was unrelenting.

"You talk the talk," Benny said, "But when Helena gave you the ash wood pendent, you said you wanted nothing to do with your father, Nolan, or your 'sister.'"

Dale stopped in his tracks, turned, and grabbed Benny by the collar with both hands. It startled Benny, and for a split second the staff fell from his grasp onto the ground. Dale's eyes flashed with the same fury Benny witnessed before Virtue's helpful bite, but Dale quickly regained composure.

"You're right, Ben. Perhaps I have demons of my own to quell. But while I still harbor negative thoughts towards Nolan—and have no desire to see him any time soon—I accepted his gift and I'm sincerely grateful to him and his daughter for helping Helena. I don't wish them harm, nor will I go out of my way to make them miserable. I simply want nothing to do with him. So think twice before opening your mouth. There was a time when I would've gladly cut your head off for what you just said." Dale winked, showing that no anger was held towards Benny, but the young man's vengeance stood firm.

"And there was a time I wouldn't have been able to stop you. But I doubt you'd be so quick to cut me down now!" Benny held out his hand and the magic staff shot up from the ground and into his hand.

The group stood still for a split second. Dale's face was contorted with a mixed look of shame at Benny's hateful remark, and shock at the act of levitation Benny had just performed.

"How'd you do that, boy?" Burgundy said as they resumed hiking.

Benny himself was somewhat perplexed. "I don't know. It just kinda happened...probably because of my emotions. My mom is a witch, after all, and she said the staff would only work for me...maybe I'm able to do things with the staff in ways I couldn't normally do, or maybe I have more magic in me than I thought."

"Don't wear yourself out figuring it out. We still have several days of the journey ahead of us," Helena stated.

So they continued marching up the mountain, until the trees gradually dispersed and the air became cooler. The next day, flora became even sparser as they approached the summit of the mountain, and soon they saw faint traces of snow along the now steep path. The side of the mountain became so steep they were forced to walk sideways, backs against the icy stone of the mountainside. They went on like this, stopping for a few hours here and there to catch their breath, but trekking on until they saw crude footsteps cut into the slope in front of them. Looking up, it seemed to Benny as if the mountain ascended forever, even into the clouds. The companions were freezing, wearing what heavy clothing they had, and they were all hesitant about the climb.

"Not much to hold on to," Helena said, "It's almost straight up into the air…more like a stone ladder."

"Well, we can't turn back now, Thunder Thighs. We wouldn't have enough rations to last us a return trip anyway." Burgundy slapped her on the butt.

Helena shot Burgundy a wicked glare and the dwarf chuckled, obviously realizing the error. Helena, who was too tired to quarrel on the mountainside, winked at him and gave him a kiss on the cheek. "I admire your persistence, but the jokes do get old after a while."

"You know you like it," Burgundy said.

With Dale taking the lead, they began the climb into the unknown.

They climbed for what seemed like an eternity, clinging to the steps on all fours as they ascended at an almost vertical angle. With his staff crudely strapped to his back, Benny took the rear, moving slowly so as to not drop his precious weapon.

"Pick up the pace, boy! You look like an ant from up here!" Burgundy's distant voice called from above.

Benny's finger's felt raw from the cold stone. They hadn't expected Alfen Gulfadex to be at the summit of a mountain; obvious as it might have seemed with the ancient city being home to the *Frost* Dwarves and all. Benny was beginning to wish they'd taken the risk of properly preparing for their journey. His mind overloaded with thought, his foot slipped on a step and he fell backwards to his death, pack, staff and all.

"Help..." Benny barely had time to call out before feeling a strong hand grab his left wrist. Looking up, Benny saw the grinning face of Quill the Sorai. Treading the air with his great wings, he pulled Benny up into a bear hug in order to transport him to the mountain summit.

"My equipment...my staff...I have to..."

"You talking about this piece of driftwood?" a voice cut Benny off. Looking to his right, Benny saw two more Sorais flying with Quill, one clutching his staff, and the other his travelling bag.

"Don't worry, kid. We gotcha covered."

In a matter of seconds, Quill pumped his wings and they shot upward. Soon, he landed, Benny in tow, on the stone ground of the mountain top. Dale and the others rushed to them.

"You're an angel, Quill...no pun intended," Benny said, shaking the winged man's hand.

Dale embraced his old rival from the tournament. "It's good to see you. I see those wings came in handy again."

After Quill introduced his companions to his fellow Sorai, named Zenith and Cloud, they turned away from the cliffside to get their first view of Alfen Gulfadex.

"And I thought the sages at Knavesmare had a kickin' pad," Burgundy said, almost speechless.

Every last structure of the city before them was comprised of pure ice. The architecture was unlike anything the companions had ever seen, which seemed to be characterized by differing sizes of spires and domes. The blue to blue-green hues of the city created a deeply calming effect as they approached the largest domed structure, which appeared to be the center of the city. As they approached the arched entrance to the building, two milk-white dwarves with equally white hair and beards appeared from inside. Ushering the companions in without a word, they followed a narrow hallway which seemed to spiral along the inside perimeter, moving inward until opening onto a large indoor amphitheater surrounded on all sides, save the entrance, by stadium seats carved into the ice itself. Benny quickly spotted an old acquaintance.

"Kolpak?" Benny asked.

The frost dwarf nodded. His beard was thicker, and his muscles stouter than they had been at the tournament in Upper Sultry where the companions had seen him last. The most obvious change, however, was the thinning hair and worry lines which wrinkled his ivory brow.

"It's good to see old friends." He glanced at Burgundy and his smile faded. "And new ones, unwelcome as they may be…Come. We have much to discuss."

They walked to the podium in the center of the room, raised several feet above the ground. A large, ceremonial quilt had been laid down in the center of the stage, sewn together with fragments of dark, earthy materials—browns, tans, and reds—with the reoccurring image of a bear-like animal embroidered in many spots. Seated in a large circle on the quilt were several dozen frost dwarves, obviously of high stature within the community. Most of them, like Kolpak, were warriors, clad in animal skins and possessing hefty war clubs and axes made from stone and animal bone. One individual, seated in the center of the circle, had wrapped himself in a thick, maroon robe and wore a headdress made from the head and pelt of a white bear the likes of which Benny had never seen before. He appeared to be deep in meditation.

"I'm fascinated by your city, Kolpak. I tried to imagine what Alfen Gulfadex would be like, but I never imagined this. A city made of ice!"

"The name *Alfen Gulfadex* literally means *City of Ice…*" Kolpak said, motioning for the companions to sit down with the other frost dwarves.

"The architecture is amazing! I would love to learn more about the history of this city, its culture, how they've managed to erect these massive, flawless buildings from pure ice." Dale, seated at the edge of the quilt, reached out and touched the icy floor of the stage, "It's ice, all right. Every bit of it is pure ice! But there's something different about it…it's not cold like ice normally is…it's…"

"Hospitable…" Burgundy said, lying back on the quilt.

"The ice is made from the magic of my people. It's an ancient process we take great pride in, and rarely do we share the secrets of our magic with outsiders. It is strong, durable, and never melts. Even in a desert, it would remain as cold and hard as it is now."

"What is this building?" Helena asked.

"It's our meeting hall…our population has dwindled through the generations. Centuries ago, our people would have filled every square inch of this auditorium," Kolpak said, his voice thick with disdain.

"And that guy…?" Benny said, pointing towards the seated figure in the middle of the room.

"He is the last shaman of our people. He has the ability of foresight, through both space and time. With enough meditation, he could describe a mating dance of the red-capped manakin of the southern jungles, or the number of bees in a hive hanging in the tree right outside your window back home. Right now, he is trying to locate the Kudgels, their numbers, and how soon they will be upon us."

"Well, what are we waiting for, dammit?" Burgundy lurched up, "Show us where yer keeping them damn horns so we can just destroy them and be done with it."

"It's not that simple," Kolpak said with a laugh.

Benny frowned. "What do you mean?"

"The horns aren't in Alfen Gulfadex."

The companions, including Quill and his brethren, were speechless. "You mean we've traveled all this way, escaped torture and death, were separated and reunited, not to mention wandering halfway across the world, to be told we're in the wrong place?" Dale was fuming.

"Calm down, Dale. I only said the horns weren't in Alfen Gulfadex. Just as there is only one path through the northern mountains to our city, there is only one path from our city to the Twin Horns."

"So we could only reach the horns once we reached Alfen Gulfadex," Benny surmised.

Kolpak smiled, "Exactly."

Dale was calmer now, but he was still antsy. "With all due respect, Kolpak, why are we just sitting here staring at some old ...dwarf?"

"Why spit into the wind?" Kolpak winked at Dale.

Dale appeared to understand, and nodded respectively.

Benny, however, was still confused. "What does that have to do with the price of beans in Gant?" he asked.

"It means that we should be patient, and wait on advice from their shaman. If we run like pigs to the slaughter, trying to find the horns in the blink of an eye, we may miss hearing crucial information that could help us." Dale stopped as the old dwarf in the center of the quilt stood up and held out his arms. What came from his mouth had Benny, as well as his friends, scratching their heads.

A string of grunts, clicks, and gulps came from the old dwarf, in what seemed more like a coughing fit than an actual language. Benny turned to Kolpak, and the frost dwarf laughed at the shared expression of the companions.

"He's very old, and doesn't know the common tongue. He only speaks the old language. He said that the Kudgels, while they know the way, have delayed in ascending the mountains, and are camped at the mouth of the pass." Kolpak turned to the dwarf as more hacks, burps, and grunts came from the shaman. The old dwarf gestured towards the companions. "He says that they will not ascend the mountains for another week at least, from which it will take them roughly a week to get here, if they can survive the terrain of the mountains. They are not aware that the horns aren't actually in this city."

"Does he know their numbers?" Helena asked.

Kolpak made equally strange noises, directed at the old shaman. They exchanged noises, and Kolpak looked back at Helena. "Only a few hundred are camped at the mountain pass, and only a few dozen of those will be ascending the mountains. However, he senses two very strong, dark entities in the group which will be trekking here."

"My mommy and bubba," Benny said.

Kolpak was confused by the statement, but continued. "He said you can afford a few days rest and recuperation from your journey, during which we will prepare you for your journey to the other side of the Northern Mountains, where the Twin Horns are located. I am to be your guide."

"There aren't gonna be any...surprises...waiting for us when we get there, are there?" Burgundy asked.

"A surprise for you, my friends, but not for me," Kolpak said.

Burgundy seemed unpleased by the statement. "What the hell is that supposed to mean?"

"A cyclops guards the horns...a REAL cyclops."

"Well, what exactly is a REAL cyclops?" Burgundy asked. "I've heard dozens of legends regarding the cyclops, and not one of 'em are the same as the next."

"The cyclops is a giant, a terrible giant, set to guard the Twin Horns by the Protector himself. In the golden age of his race, it is said that even the Sky Titans feared them," Kolpak said.

"Why did the Protector have the cyclops guard the horns?" Dale asked.

"It's a long story, so I'll start with the beginning. When the Protector came to what is now Pakk, it was a barren wasteland, void of life or any way to support life. So he created the skies and the oceans, the forests, jungles, mountains, savannas, and more. He created wildlife, every fowl of the air, every animal on land, and fish in the sea. Then, he created the first intelligent life to set foot on Pakk, which he called the Guardians. These beings, who would become the Sky Titans, were tremendous in size and knowledge...second only to the Protector himself. They were created to love and care for the races of intelligent beings which were created after them. However, over the centuries that followed, the original races which would become humans, dwarves, halflings, elves, giants, and countless others, slowly changed from the peaceful, innocent creation they were intended to be. They turned away from the Protector and the guidance of his Guardians, and at first, sought mere independence. Independence led to greed, malice, lust, and soon the Protector's creation was almost unrecognizable."

"Why didn't this Protector just start over? Just wipe the slate clean, or make his creation mind him? Doesn't make much sense to me," Burgundy said.

"Because of his love. The Protector wanted his creation to follow him not because they were forced to, but because they wanted to. He probably could have created the world and this life in a way that evil would never have existed. But then we would be slaves, forced to do good for lack of anything else. The Protector wanted his creation to think for themselves, decide for themselves, and so he and the Guardians agreed to give the races the independence they so desired, and the Guardians agreed to part from Pakk, and take their abode in the sky and in the clouds above us, to wait until they were needed once again. And so, the Protector crafted with his own hands two horns, one of silver and one of gold, and placed them in the north, beyond the mountains, to be used if the world ever became overrun with evil to the point that good was almost extinguished. In this case, the Gold Horn was to be blown to summon the Guardians, the Sky Titans, in order to destroy the world, wiping it clean of all evil and allowing the Protector start anew."

"What is the Silver Horn for?" Benny asked.

"In case, for any reason, one wished to call off the Sky Titans, and thus save the world from destruction. The

Protector knew of the troubles which would plague Pakk in the future, and that people would attempt to summon the Sky Titans 'pre-maturely,' either by accident or ill intention. Therefore, he placed one of his most powerful creatures, a cyclops, in charge of guarding the horns. This way, only those with the most sincere of intentions towards blowing the Golden Horn, and summoning the Sky Titans, could defeat the cyclops."

"Well, if this cyclops thing is guarding the horns and only those with good intentions can defeat him, what are we even going to all this damn trouble for? I could be back at home sleeping!" Burgundy crossed his arms and pouted.

"I said *sincere* intentions, not *good* intentions," Kolpak stated. There had been tension between the two dwarves ever since they'd met, but now it had become an obvious thorn in each other's side.

"Sincere…good…same damn difference!"

Helena cut off Burgundy, "Not quite, lover boy. Someone sincerely wanting to blow the horns doesn't have to have good intentions. People like Ammarod and Benny's mother sincerely want to blow the horns for their own evil purposes. Their desire to summon the Titans is just as strong as our desire to do the opposite."

"And we still don't know the full extent of their power…" Benny said.

The companions agreed in unison. The shaman made more noise, even louder and more emphatic than before. Kolpak translated. "He says the mother is more powerful, but the son is the one we should fear…" Kolpak stared at Benny, and the companions followed suit.

"What? What are you looking at me for?" he asked.

Kolpak responded. "He also said that you, and only you, were the one who could defeat him…with your skill alone."

Benny's stomach lurched. He'd grown worlds since his childhood as the clumsy, backwards boy he'd been when he first met Dale and Cycleze, but when he thought back to all of his battles, he'd always had some form of outside help. Virtue had bit him with a berserker bite in his battle against the evil Dale, Marty had saved him from assassination, and he'd had the combined aid of Helena and Dale in full berserk mode in his fight against Purp. He did slay Toldnas the Giant with his magic staff during his feast with the Emperor of Upper Sultry, but he'd only been able to do so because the giant was distracted by his feuding with Dale, Quill, and the other tournament winners. He was ten times the fighter and adventurer he'd been when first traveling across Dan with Dale those years ago, but he'd never truly been alone. As angry as he was towards his brother for what he'd done to Virtue, and as resentful as he was towards his mother for her abandonment and evil ways, he was still unsure of himself in comparison to them. He was still afraid.

"That's nonsense," Dale said.

Kolpak shook his head. "I'm sorry, lad. Only Benny can stop his brother. The shaman is never wrong."

"Never?" It was more of a plea from Benny than a question.

"Never," the dwarf stated.

With that, the shaman made a final declaration, and the gathering of frost dwarves slowly began to depart. Benny, Dale, and the rest of the travelers followed Kolpak to their designated quarters to prepare for the next leg of the journey.

It was spring time in Dan and the crabapples were bursting with white and pink blossoms. The orchard was a special place for Laurel and her betrothed, the gentle Ammarod, and on many a summer afternoon they made love beneath the trees, and this sunset was no exception. His blue skin against hers, the warmth of the sun on their bodies, and the honeysuckle scent of the apple blossoms engulfing her senses; Laurel was lost in him. Then it happened. A dark cloud cut off the peaceful rays of the sun, the air became cold and dry, and the mist came upon the lovers, choking them. Then the vampires came; wicked evil creatures, like bats out of hell, erupting from the ground itself. One bit hard into Laurel's neck, knocking her back. She watched in horror, frozen in agony from the bite, as they descended on her Ammarod. Blood spewed into the air, flesh and limbs were torn from his body, and his screams echoed throughout the countryside. That's when she came. A demoness, clothed in moss and smelling like the musk of decaying earth, her skin pale, dead, and her eyes black like onyx. Her teeth were razors, and her fingernails knives. She gave out a cry as she came into the scene, diving into the cluster of feeding vampires. Laurel was terrified for her lover, but as his blood sprayed into the air and flowed upon the ground she realized it was too late, and her own physical condition too weak anyway. So, using what ability she had, she fled through the orchard and into the surrounding forest. She ran until her lungs were bursting. Collapsing onto the ground, she passed out. The last thing she heard was Ammarod's scream.

Virtue had indeed been Laurel. While she had never shared the true story of her conversion with Benny, it was a moment that haunted her always. She had been taken in by a peaceful group of vampires, who chased off attackers, and they took her to their home in the Gant countryside. She had begged them to look for Ammarod, but, upon returning, claimed only a puddle of blood remained of her beloved. Every day, she had remembered Ammarod, the gentle, blue-skinned farm boy, whom many had shunned but she embraced for his kindness and intelligence. The reason she had fallen in love with Benny had been because he'd reminded her so much of Ammarod; he had

Ammarod's gentle innocence, his goofiness, and his perseverance...even his looks resembled Ammarod, apart from the hair and skin. Benny knew about their past now, at least on a general basis, and while Magenta had helped her reunite with Benny for a moment, she was still worried about the events to come.

"Virtue," a voice called her back to reality as a green hand rested on her shoulder.

Virtue placed her own hand on Bum's calloused fingers. "Oh goodness! I'm so sorry, Bum."

The noise of the evening regulars in the bar returned to her consciousness. She had taken a break from waitressing and bartending and sat in a cubby behind the bar. "Why don't you go get some rest? You don't look so well."

"No," she said, standing up, "I think it'd be better to stay busy...keep my mind off things. An idle mind wouldn't help me much right now."

She moved among the patrons, taking orders, fetching drinks and the usual, but her mind was constantly drawn back to Ammarod, who he once was and what he'd become. Her respite with Benny, which she had expected to heal her troubled mind, now seemed like a distant memory. Then it came, that musky scent of old: wet earth, moss, smoke. She heard the tavern doors open and felt the room grow cold as a robed figure stepped into the room. The jovial voices of the patrons grew hollow, their movements screeching to a halt in mid-air. Virtue knew the woman behind the robe.

"It's obvious enough who you are. Knock off the parlor tricks," Virtue said. She was taken back at the brashness of her own voice. *Dale's rubbing off on me*, she thought to herself.

Black tipped fingers revealed themselves from the dark, gauzy sleeves and pulled back her hood. The pentagram tattooed on her face was new, but the dark eyes, razor teeth, and icy blue lips were just as Virtue had remembered them. "You have something that belongs to me, Virtue...or should I say, Laurel." She smiled, revealing her mouth of daggers.

"I own nothing of any value to you. I know the power you have, and anything in my possession would be useless to you, witch."

"I'm not talking about books, potions, or charms, stupid girl. You've taken something I can never get back..." There was sorrow in the witch's voice, despite her wickedness. "...You stole my children's hearts."

Virtue was confused by her words, and made no connection as to who these "children" could be. "Benny?" she whispered.

"And another. One whose fate was meant for you," she said.

Virtue's heart plunged into her stomach. "Ammarod! You are the mother of Ammarod and my Benny. They're brothers!" While she had shared her rape with Benny, and some broad details of her past with Ammarod, Benny had not told her of his connection with Ammarod or this woman.

"I love all my children, little wench, and it hurts a mother to see her sons give love meant for her to one like you. Yes, I am responsible for what happened to Ammarod. My servants were meant to kill you, and bring my son to me. I should've known better then to trust hungry, fresh-turned vampires with the task. But I have made up for my mistake tenfold...I gave Ammarod a new body, added a few of the noble features of the Kudgel race, and made him the mightiest leader this world has ever seen. I have taught him the magic of absorbing souls, and he has inherited the ability to dematerialize into smoke...very similar to the skills of my beloved Benny."

"You are some witch indeed, for Ammarod to follow you after what you did to him."

At this statement, the witch frowned. "He doesn't know, and he isn't going to find out. He thinks I rescued him. I slaughtered and ate the vampires who attacked him...he was barely alive when I found him, his limbs torn from his body and entrails strewn through the orchard like garlands of holly in winter time. I healed him the best I could, but in the end created the new body he has now." The witch grinned. "I'm sure you got to experience it. No thanks required."

"You can't control what he's become," Virtue declared.

"And I don't intend to. Even now, I have the power to kill Ammarod in an instant, although I'd never raise a hand against my children...at least not to kill them. I do, however, have no qualms about killing you!"

"Why did you do it, witch? Why did you destroy what we had...why are you doing the same now with Benny?"

She cackled, "Do call me Winona, little bat. I would at least like you to know the name of the one killing you. As to your question, I already told you. I've kept an eye on all my children, though I felt it best not to interfere with their lives for some time. However, I grew to miss them terribly...then I noticed how attached Ammarod had grown to you. It enraged me to see him love you so dearly, love that should have been mine. I gave birth to him, and to Benny and Aiken! They are mine, and belong to me! I will not have the likes of you stealing their affection."

"You abandoned them! Ammarod never knew his mother, and neither did Benny. Not to mention his father dying at a young age, and Aiken abandoning him. If you wanted their love, you had to have actually been there to experience that love."

Winona shrugged. "You might be right. Perhaps I should have given up my black magic, settled down and raised a family, but it's not my way. I go with the flow of the wind, the tremble of the earth, and the rolling of the rivers."

"You're helplessly messed up," Virtue said.

"I always was the jealous type. I will, of course, lie to Benny about your death...perhaps blame it on my soldiers, or some ailment. I can't have my son thinking any worse about me than he already does. I'd like to tell you it's not personal...but that would be a lie."

Virtue tried to move, but couldn't. While her consciousness had been spared by the spell, physically she was as frozen as the other bar patrons. She knew and could feel the power building in the witch, and knew her death would come swiftly if she didn't act. There was a spell she'd studied only briefly, but it was her only chance of combating Winona's power.

"Do what you feel is necessary, Winona," Virtue said.

A single, bloody tear streamed from Winona's eye. "I *will* have my family back!"

She rushed at Virtue and, in an instant, it was over.

Chapter 10
The Horns

Benny was glad for several days of rest and comfort, enjoying the surprisingly warm hospitality of the frost dwarves. But this reprieve also gave him time to think about being alone. Dale had Helena, and Burgundy had his lascivious dreams, but Benny slept by himself. He missed Virtue, and wanted to sleep in her arms again. That also reminded him of Magenta, who had animated Virtue for a night with him. There was a trace of guilt there; had it been only his wife he appreciated? He had known it was Magenta hosting Virtue, and maybe there had been some feeling for Magenta herself, pretty enough and surely a worthy woman. She had played the role perfectly. How could he be sure exactly whom he was really kissing, in his fancy? It wasn't that he didn't love Virtue, just that there might be an admixture of something else.

Helena took one look at him. "Magenta! I must play the flute."

Benny looked at her blankly. His expression had reminded her of Magenta?

"Magenta gave me a flute," she explained. "It will alert her to our arrival here, so she can join us. It is time."

Benny felt a glad thrill. Then he stifled it as his guilt welled up. "Why should Magenta join us here?"

"She is part of the denouement. We need her."

"Need her for what?" He was arguing the case as much with himself as with her. "She has the Kudgels to pacify; she is surely busy."

Helena pondered momentarily. "I am not completely clear on that. I just know that she has to be with us. But it may take a few days for her to get here. She has to find the right teleportation stone."

Benny was relieved and disappointed. If Magenta came here, Virtue could animate her and he could kiss her. If that was really all he wanted. At least he would not be put to that test right now.

The Amazon produced a small wood flute. "I have never been much of a musician, but I suppose music is not the point here. I just need to blow it, I think."

"Yes," Benny agreed.

She put the flute to her mouth and blew. A lovely melody emerged. Surprised, she stopped, looking at it suspiciously. "I just blew."

"You must have more musical talent than you thought."

"But I wasn't even trying to play it, just to make a note." She tried again, and more appealing music came. Benny could see that her fingers weren't covering the keys; it was indeed magic.

Helena stopped and put it away. "That must suffice."

Now, several dwarves had gathered, including the leader, Kolpak. "You have unsuspected talent," he remarked appreciatively.

"The flute does, anyway," she agreed wryly.

Well rested, they girded themselves for the journey. Kolpak and several frost dwarves led the way to a secret path only they knew that would take them to the horns. The Sorai flew closely overhead, high enough to see the route, low enough so as not to be too visible from afar, lest the path lose its secrecy.

The shaman jerked awake with an exclamation of alarm, but before the dwarves could run to help him, they were struck by a deadly smoke that cloaked their heads and choked them to death. Then the smoke surrounded the shaman and, in moments, he too was dead.

The smoke cleared to reveal two figures: Ammarod Current and the witch, Winona. "Do you have him, son?" she asked.

"I have his soul," Current said. "That's enough. We now know the secret path."

"That will do," she agreed. She lifted her voice slightly. "Here to me, folk."

Several Kudgels appeared, led by the Grand Hydra. They had hidden until the witch accomplished what was necessary. Now they had the information they needed, and were on their way.

The route was treacherous for anyone not in the know about its pitfalls; Benny appreciated that in passing. They had traversed it, but would need guidance again to return along it. No one would be able to pursue them here. Even the two winged warriors, the Sorai, would have trouble without the guide.

Yet somehow, he had a nasty feeling about it.

They reached a high glade whose perimeter dropped off precipitously. "This is it," Kolpak announced.

"This is too easy," Dale muttered.

"There has to be a catch," Helena agreed.

There were the Twin Horns. They were mounted on huge stone pedestals, and were jewel encrusted. One was silver, the other gold. Benny knew that the Gold Horn was the one that would summon the Sky Titans. The one not to blow.

But they did not have time to linger in admiration. The Cyclops emerged from a shrouded cave. He was twenty feet tall and massive in proportion; the ground shook with his tread. His huge, single eye glared down at them. "You seek the horns?" he demanded. "Before you touch them, you must defeat me in combat."

"But this isn't supposed to be a combat mission," Dale protested. "We are here on behalf of the Planet of Pakk, to make sure the horns don't get blown."

"No one has anything to do with the horns without first settling with me," the Cyclops declared. "Now fight or flee before I throw you off the mountain."

"But we come in peace," Helena said. "We don't want to fight you, but we won't flee."

"Only a force that can defeat me in combat is worthy enough to blow the horns," the Cyclops said, eyeing her with a certain muted appreciation. "Prove yourselves, or get out."

"Damn," Dale said. "We can't risk leaving the horns for the Kudgels to take. We'll have to settle with him." He drew his sword.

"It's nothing personal," Helena said, drawing hers. Benny, Burgundy, Kolpak, and the dwarves followed suit. They were many to the monster's one, but the Cyclops probably outweighed them all and was obviously a seasoned warrior. This would not be easy.

Benny's misgivings continued. He feared they were fighting a friend rather than an enemy. Then he got a notion. "Wait!" he cried. "We're not enemies! We're contestants. We can determine the victor without bloodshed. We need dull swords."

The others looked at him as if he were crazy. "How can we do that?" Dale asked incredulously.

But the Cyclops understood. "Rub that rock," he said, indicating a dark slab set into the mountain slope. "So." He demonstrated, rubbing one side of his huge blade on the stone. It came away dark and looked dull. Then he rubbed the other side. Then he chopped at a branch. Instead of cutting it off, the blade bounced. It was dull and maybe cushioned, so that while it could bash, it couldn't cut.

The Cyclops stepped back, waiting on them.

Helena shook her head, bemused. "Out of the mouths of babies," she murmured, and rubbed her sword. The others followed, including Zenith and Cloud.

"I hope there's an antidote," Kolpak muttered as he stroked his weapon.

"The other stone," the Cyclops said, gesturing to a similar slab across the glade.

The fight resumed. The first to engage the Cyclops were the two Sorai. The one-eyed giant swept his sword across, catching them in its arc and smashing them to the ground. They were uninjured, but shaken and out of the fight for now. It seemed that the blade was not only blunted, but softened so as not to cause a club-like injury.

Dale and Helena attacked together, striking at the knees, which were as tall as they were. "Ooo!" the Cyclops howled as bruises appeared. The dulled blades did have some punch. Then he kicked out with both feet, a feat impossible to most folk, and swept them to the side. Like the Sorai, they were not technically injured, but would take a while to recover.

The dwarves swarmed the feet, bashing at the toes. "Ooo!" the Cyclops repeated as his feet bruised. He tried to kick the dwarves away, but they were on top of the feet and clinging to them, refusing to be dislodged. He squatted and brought his sword down to knock them off.

At this point, Benny dropped his sword and invoked his staff. He leaped onto the Cyclops' bent knee, and leaped again, smacking the staff against the giant eyeball. He felt its magic working.

"OOOOO!" the Cyclops screamed, falling back on his rear. "I'm blinded!"

"Have we proved ourselves?" Benny called. "Do you yield?"

The Cyclops nodded. "I yield. You are worthy."

Helena stepped up. "You have healing elixir? Where is it?"

"In the cave, Amazon," he said, evidently recognizing her voice.

She went to the cave and returned with a double armful of white paste. "Is this it?" She threw a glob at the damaged eye.

The glob struck, spread out, and sank into the flesh. The eye blinked, then brightened. The Cyclops could see again. "Yes," he said belatedly.

"Friends?" Helena asked.

"Yes. Kiss me, Amazon."

She laughed and sat on his extended hand. He brought her to his face and she kissed his nose.

"That makes it worth it," he said as he set her carefully down.

After that, they were indeed friends. The copious salve repaired all of their bruises and restored their vitality.

They stroked their weapons against the other stone, restoring their sharpness, then joined the Cyclops in his cave, which turned out to be remarkably comfortable and well appointed. He served dishes of tasty stew and they talked.

"We're actually here to destroy the horns," Benny said cautiously, afraid this would make them enemies again.

"That's good," the Cyclops said. "Those horns are sheer mischief and should be abolished."

Had he heard correctly? "But you are guarding them!"

"I am guarding them from those who would abuse their powers. That's my assignment. That doesn't mean I like it."

All of them gazed at the Cyclops. "This is of the nature of a private opinion," Dale said. "Separate from your duty."

"Exactly. I would be quite satisfied to see them abolished. Then my onerous mission would be finished and I could go home."

"If you feel that way," Helena said, "Why didn't you destroy them yourself? That would prevent anyone from abusing their powers, so is consistent with your mission."

"I can't. They are almost invulnerable."

"So we have come here for nothing?" Benny asked, irritated.

"Not at all. I can't touch them, but you can."

"Why should I want to? To blow one could be doom."

The Cyclops looked at him. "You hold the only weapon that can damage them."

"I do?" Benny asked, surprised again.

"You brought it here coincidentally?"

"Maybe the Protector directed it," Benny said thoughtfully.

"That must be the case. He set me to guard them, and you to destroy them."

Benny looked at his staff. "I had no idea!" He looked around. "Then maybe we'd better get to it."

But then they all froze in place, except for the Cyclops. Benny could move his eyes to look, but that was all. What was happening?

A black cloud floated into the cave. No, it was some kind of fuzzy air ship, supporting two people and several Kudgels. It settled onto the floor, and the two got off. Benny saw with astonishment that they were his mother Winona and his brother Ammarod Current. They had used magic transportation to get here unexpectedly rapidly. But how had they known the way?

Winona faced the Cyclops. "Where do you stand, One-Eye?" she demanded.

The giant hesitated. "I discover that I am not allowed to intervene in your affairs," he said after a moment. "I do not understand this, but it is so."

"Then you are dismissed," the witch said.

Benny was amazed. The Cyclops was permitting this? How could that be?

The Cyclops glanced at Benny as if understanding his question. "This turns out to be a more complicated situation than I can handle," he said. "I must let it play out in its own fashion." He departed.

"Indeed," Winona said.

"What is complicated?" Ammarod asked her. "We are here to blow the Horn."

"No. That is the final expedient if we fail our primary mission."

"Our allies are turning against us. This signals incipient failure. That is why we must destroy the present system."

"We can recover our allies," Winona said. "The key is Magenta, who is marshaling the leading contingent."

"Magenta," Ammarod said. "She is a lot of woman, willful and physically appealing. I mean to have her for my concubine, though I may have to manacle her hands and feet and file off her teeth to inhibit her resistance. Even so, it may be a challenge to possess her. But she will never return that contingent to us."

"Not if treated like that," Winona agreed. "That's why you can't have her."

Ammarod laughed. "What is the point in killing her? She is too good to waste."

"She will not be wasted. The key to her cooperation lies with Benny."

Benny, still in stasis, was startled. Was this the reason Magenta was to come to join them? But he would never ask her to turn her contingent of Kudgels over to the enemy.

"We must persuade her to join us," Winona said. "That is what Benny can do. She likes him, and may soon love him, now that the way has been cleared. For him, she may turn that corner."

This was another surprise for Benny. Magenta liked him? She had been good to him, certainly, but he had never fooled himself that this was anything more than her niceness as a person and friendship with Virtue. And what was this about the way being cleared?

"Mother, Benny is warring against us," Ammarod reminded her. "He is not about to change sides either."

"That remains to be seen. I have been guiding him indirectly all his life. Now it is time to become direct."

"I don't understand," Ammarod said.

Neither did Benny. What was the woman up to?

"I have an ambition of my own," Winona said. "I want to be queen of Pakk, with my sons as regent kings. This requires intricate management."

Ammarod shrugged. "You can be queen, of course, and I will be a king, if we conquer the planet. What does Benny have to do with that?"

"He is my son, as are you. I am the only woman who has truly cared for either of you. It has been an ongoing challenge to protect the two of you from heartache."

"The two of us?" Ammarod asked. "I am not aware of this."

"Of course you aren't. I was not certain that either of you would properly understand my efforts."

"What efforts?" Ammarod demanded. Benny was curious too.

"My efforts to prevent you from being corrupted by scheming women."

"*What* scheming women?"

Winona hesitated, then evidently decided to say something she hadn't planned on. "Laurel, for one thing."

Benny remembered that that was her name for Virtue Vampire. But Virtue was no schemer. Far from it! She was a completely lovable partner and wife.

"Laurel!" Ammarod said. "I loved her!"

"Exactly," Winona said evenly. "She was casting her wicked spell, taking you away from me. I had to act. She finally died the way she was supposed to."

Benny suffered an ugly chill. Virtue was dead?

"What do you mean, the way she was supposed to?" Ammarod demanded. At this point, Benny was with him. "She was never wicked. She was a lovely, innocent girl, a considerable change of pace from the females I have known."

"Yes. The others were sluts and you knew it and used them accordingly. No problem there. But Laurel was winning your heart and soul. She forced my hand early."

"Forced your hand? We were attacked by vampires!"

"Not exactly, son. I sent my servants, who were freshly turned vampires, to kill Laurel, ending that threat, and bring you back to me. But they attacked you instead, tearing your limbs from your body, strewing your entrails across the land, gang-biting you, feeding on your precious blood, while she managed to get away, albeit as a converted vampire. She had, I think, no proper memory of the occasion, and thought she had turned vampire voluntarily. Neither did you. I could not repair your body from their feeding frenzy, so I created a new and better body for you, the one you have now."

Benny was appalled. He had had no idea that Virtue had been converted by force, and it seemed she didn't either. All because Ammarod's mother was jealous of his affection for Laurel!

Ammarod was so tight he was like a statue. He, too, had not known. "You intended to kill Laurel? The woman I loved?"

"Son, I didn't want to tell you, but it was the only way! Her memory of you was returning. She was ensnaring your heart. I had to act."

"And how did she finally die?" His words were barely audible.

"Seeing there was no other way, I took personal charge so there would be no further mistakes. I finally visited her at the home she shared with Benny, in her guise of Virtue. She was ensnaring you a second time, after completely corrupting Benny. You thought you were raping her, but you were doing only what she compelled you to do. You could not help yourself. You thought you were possessing her, but she was possessing you. So I knifed her to death, making sure there could be no recovery."

Ammarod was silent. Benny shared his horror.

"And thus, I cleared the way for Magenta," Winona concluded. "She is no vampire and is not a schemer. She is truly innocent of the female machinations. She can be managed. She can take Laurel's place with Benny, and when he has won her love, we can slowly turn her to our side. We will win back the rogue Kudgel contingent. We will win the planet. I will be queen, and you and Benny will be kings. That is why you must not touch her again, son. You abused her, and she will never trust you the way she will trust Benny. This way is perfect."

"You're mad," Ammarod whispered. Benny could not have said it better.

"Not at all, son. I am practical. I am doing what needs to be done, and I know you and Benny will appreciate that in due course."

"Because of you, I lost Laurel and turned to the dark side," Ammarod said in a low tone. "I thought Laurel had abandoned me, and turned to Benny to spite me. That's why I treated her roughly when I found her in her new alias. I lost everything I really cared about, including Laurel's love."

"Yes. Isn't it wonderful? Now you can start over, unencumbered emotionally. You can be mine again."

"I lost everything," Ammarod repeated. "Including, now, my mother."

"No, my dear, you have at last recovered her."

Ammarod drew a knife and leaped for her before she could react. He stabbed her repeatedly. She cried out, not with pain, but surprise. In her insanity, she had never anticipated this.

Ammarod turned away, leaving her to die. As Winona's life faded, her spell of stasis wore off, and Benny and the others recovered their ability to move.

Benny ran to her. "I'm sorry!" he cried. Despite her crimes, he knew she had done it from love, not hate. Cruelly twisted, but nevertheless love.

"Benny," she gasped. "I will always love you, Ammarod, and Aiken. All I wanted was for the three of you to be with me."

"It didn't have to be like this!" Benny cried.

"I knew no other way," she said, stroking his face. She smiled weakly. "You look just like your father."

Then, she died as he held her. Her body transformed from the demonic witch into a beautiful young lady. That had to be her suppressed inner soul.

Benny rose to confront Ammarod, determined to set things straight. The others stood by, not interfering. Could this have been the reason the Cyclops had had to depart? To let this vital sequence play out? "I understand you better than I did before," Benny said. "I share some of your horror. But you need to know that Virtue still cared for you, when she remembered, even though you ravished her. You did her an injustice. I don't hold you responsible for the brainwashing by our mother, Winona. Do not misjudge Magenta similarly; she is no proper part of that plot." He hoped his half-brother would heed his words, because otherwise there would be more blood to shed.

Ammarod remained stoic, not speaking.

"There is a way to end the war," Benny continued. "Both in Pakk and in your heart. This world is governed by the Protector, and he has allowed me to speak for him in this respect. He will forgive you if you change your ways and recant what you have done."

Now Ammarod spoke. "It is too late. There is no other way."

Dale intervened. "I was just like you, Ammarod, and probably worse, until Virtue saved me. It's never too late."

Ammarod was silent, but a single tear streamed down his otherwise emotionless face.

Benny tried one last time to turn his brother. "The Horns are to summon the Sky Titans. They will destroy everything, including us. There will be nothing left."

"I know," Ammarod said.

Benny was desperate. "Then what do you want out of this?"

"The end." Then Ammarod attacked.

The Kudgels sprang into action, going after Dale, Helena, and Burgundy. The three were ready for them. This had been a pause, not a truce.

That left Benny to deal with Ammarod. He had tried to make peace, but underneath it lay his anger over what the man had done to Virtue and planned to do to Magenta. Now that his brother had rejected the offer, Benny was free to pursue the other course. To destroy him.

If Ammarod was surprised by Benny's ferocity, he didn't show it. He skillfully fended off Benny's attack, and countered with his own thrusts. There was to be no easy victory here for either man.

The others made short work of the Kudgels, sending the survivors fleeing back up into the mountain. They came to watch Benny and Ammarod fight, not interfering. Benny heard their comments as if he were a spectator, but he was not distracted. He pressed his attack unrelentingly, using his staff rather than his sword. It was as if he had two sides, the Peacemaker and the Warrior. The first had failed; now it was the second's turn.

"They're moving so fast I can barely see them," Dale said, impressed.

"Ammarod looks like black smoke, and Benny's ghosting causes him to look like a blur," Helena agreed.

"I couldn't fight better in my dreams," Burgundy said. That was a significant compliment, considering.

But Ammarod was no pushover. He was clearly as proficient against a staff as a sword or other weapon. He feinted, and managed to catch his blade against the staff next to Benny's hand. Benny had to let go lest his fingers get sliced off, and the staff flung out and away. Benny himself was knocked back, for the moment disoriented.

Ammarod did not follow up against Benny. Instead, moving as smoke, he attacked the companions. Caught unprepared, they were vulnerable. In moments, Kolpak's soldiers were killed, and so were Quill's Sorai companions. Then he turned on Quill and Kolpak, quickly injuring and disarming them.

"Hey!" Dale exclaimed, raising his sword, about to go into berserker mode. But Ammarod bashed him back, and knocked out Helena before she could react. They were sucker punches in effect, but they were the suckers.

It occurred to Benny that Ammarod had not been trying to kill him, but to engage him long enough to divert the others so he could wipe them out by surprise. That devious ploy had worked. They had misjudged the man's deadly cunning.

Benny drew his sword and charged back into the fray. Ammarod, finally winded from his extraordinary combat, collapsed beside the Golden Horn. He must have drawn on special resources, which were now exhausted, leaving him depleted and vulnerable.

Benny hesitated. Did he really want to smash his brother now while he was down? Maybe the man would finally surrender.

Ammarod caught the Golden Horn, put it to his mouth, and blew it. It made a loud, bellowing noise that echoed throughout the countryside.

Benny realized that he had been suckered again. Ammarod had feigned exhaustion so as to get close to the Horn. Then, while Benny paused, he had acted.

Furious, Benny swung his sword, aiming to decapitate the man. But Ammarod smoked out, the sword passing harmlessly through his neck. He had been ready for this, too. The man was not merely a superior fighter, he was a devastating strategist. He had Benny figured every which way.

Then he came at Benny, ready to suffocate him in his deadly vapor and capture his soul. Benny reversed the ploy, ghosting in that instant. This time, he didn't merely return to solid substance a moment later. He focused on the enemy, taking him in while he was vapor. Then Benny materialized, holding that smoke within him.

Ammarod had tried in effect to eat him. Instead, he had eaten Ammarod.

"Where is he?" Dale asked, fearful of another deadly ploy.

"I ate him," Benny said.

"You what?"

"I incorporated his vapor into my substance. He is now part of me, and completely subject to my will."

"I didn't know you could do that!"

"Neither did I," Benny said, surprised. "I am still learning my abilities."

Helena recovered. "You're some man."

Then, Burgundy spied something. "You missed his head. It's lying there behind you."

They all looked. There was the head. Benny realized that Ammarod had been in motion, and the head must have been just beyond Benny when he materialized. He had caught everything except that.

But first they had to deal with the Horn. The message of the first could be countered by the second, if blown in time. Dale took the Silver Horn and blew a blast.

"Now destroy them both," Dale told Benny. "Before there can be any more mischief."

Benny recovered his staff and used it to attack the Horns. A beam of light emerged that cracked them both. They were now useless, as they could no longer be blown.

There was laughter. It was Ammarod's head, magically animated.

Kolpak confronted the head. "What are you laughing about, since in moment you will be all the way dead without your body?"

"It is because I know something you don't, you fools."

"What is that?" Benny asked suspiciously.

"When I absorbed the frost dwarf shaman's soul, I learned which horn summoned the Titans and which one called them off," the head said. Somehow it made sounds without having any air. "It is the Silver Horn that summons the Titans, and the Gold Horn that calls them off, not the other way around. In his old age the shaman made a blunder. I was going to blow the Silver Horn next, but you did it for me. The Titans are coming! What a laugh!"

The others gazed at each other with horror. Could this be true?

The head became serious. "Benny, I admire your strength. You fought well on every level and are a worthy brother. Maybe you will find a way to weasel out of this disaster too. But be warned: there will be others worse than me, who won't be tempered by being related to you. Your most serious challenge is still ahead of you."

This abrupt compliment and warning overcame Benny. He had on one level wanted to make up with his brother, and now it was happening, but too late. He felt tears starting. The others were silent, staying tactfully out of it. Someone drew him in comfortingly.

"My residual magic is expiring," Ammarod's head said. "I am finally truly dying. For what it's worth, I'm sorry it had to be this way. And I'm sorry about Laurel. She was a better woman than I believed." Then his eyes closed, and the head dissolved into a puddle of goo. He was gone.

"And for what little else it's worth," Dale said, "I think he meant it."

"I'm sure he did," Helena said. Benny discovered that she was the one holding him. Noting his dawning dismay, she said, "Desdemona Dryad made me do it. I'm wearing her pendant, and sometimes it takes over. She doesn't like to let folk suffer." She disengaged and stepped back.

Oh. She had mentioned the amulet she wore. Desdemona was the dryad Nolan Ducat had married, then lost. She was clearly a good soul, literally. "Uh, thanks," he said.

"Ammarod said worse is coming," Dale said. "He must mean the Sky Titans. It seems they have been summoned after all, as Ammarod said."

"We had better get back to Alfen Gulfadex," Helena said. "To warn them."

"Only Kolpak knows the route," Burgundy reminded them.

"I will guide you back immediately," Kolpak agreed grimly.

They gathered up their gear and made ready to travel.

Then there was a distraction. They saw multiple beams of green light shooting down in the forest beyond the ruined Horns. "What is that?" Helena asked, alarmed.

"We'll check," Kolpak said. "We don't want to take the path with an unknown menace following us. It may be a natural phenomenon." He and Quill went into the woods to find out what was happening.

The remaining four walked to the edge of the glade where the path took off and waited. "Think we should have gone with them?" Dale asked.

"They know this area better than we do," Helena said. "We'd only get in the way."

"I've got a bad feeling about this," Burgundy said. "Those light beams aren't anything natural, and Kolpak knew it. He was just trying to reassure us."

Benny had to agree. His body was assimilating the portion of Ammarod he had absorbed, and though the head had not been included, the body had some knowledge of its own. It was nervous about the green light.

There was a loud roar that shook the ground around them. Then Kolpak ran out of the woods, covered in blood. "Run!" he screamed.

Behind him, Quill, his wings completely ripped off, staggered into the open just as an enormous green hand reached through the trees and grabbed him. At least a dozen giants, even larger than the Cyclops, broke into the opening.

Each was around thirty feet tall, with green skin and long, green hair and beard.

The giant holding Quill lifted the struggling man up to his face as if to look at him more closely. Then, to Benny's utter shock, he shoved Quill into his mouth and bit off his head. He threw the body into the distance.

The Sky Titans had arrived.

Chapter 11
Magenta

The Sky Titans wasted no time on formalities. One of the giants shouted, "I'll eat you, little man!" and charged, spitting fire from his mouth and lightning bolts from his fingertips. The others spread out, attacking the countryside and setting everything on fire.

There was nothing to do but flee.

"This way!" Kolpak said, leading them into the path.

They dived after him. The Titans, surprisingly, did not immediately follow. "That path is masked," Kolpak explained. "They can't see it. But they surely know where Alfen Gulfadex is. We must get there first."

Benny heard the crashing of branches and trees, felt the heat of the fires, and needed no further encouragement to move out. It was a hurried trip, but they all were strongly motivated and familiar with the procedure if not the actual route. They reached the city in good time.

But news had already gotten there. The dwarves were fighting more of the Titans. There was no time to prepare a defense, assuming that was even possible; the disaster was upon them.

"Damn!" Benny swore, striking the staff into the ground. Was this the end, simply because they hadn't quite stopped the Horns from getting blown? It seemed unfair. "Why do you allow this, Protector?" he cried. "This is not fair to any of the good people who never sought such mischief!"

A shadow fell across him. The figure of a Titan loomed, large even for that form. "Who stomps the staff?" a voice boomed.

Benny was beyond patience. "Who wants to know?" he demanded.

The figure squatted down before him. Now Benny saw that it was almost twice the size of the other Titans, and royally garbed. "It is I, Tybalt, King of the Titans," he said. "My name means 'leader of the people,' but that has nothing to do with you inferior creatures. The time has finally come for me to destroy the little men, and I relish the occasion. It has been far too long in coming." He formed a fireball in his huge hands, so big it could have swallowed Benny without flickering. "Now answer me, you who hold the staff that has been lost for centuries, only to appear now to ruin the Horns. Who are you, and how did you manage to steal so precious an artifact?"

Benny was daunted. The King of the Titans! But he answered. "I am Benny Clout, well-meaning mortal. I stole nothing! I won the staff as a prize in a contest, and am still learning how to use it. Why do you care?"

"I care because, though I do not value the rest of the planet, I do value the staff. You possess it as stolen goods. I want to return it to my museum collection. But the enchantment on it defends the one it—in its inanimate ignorance—supposes is its legitimate associate. I can't destroy you without destroying it, which would be an annoying waste. So it seems I must acquire it from you before I destroy your world, nuisance as that may be. What is your price?"

Benny looked at the staff. He had had no idea! "I didn't know it was stolen. If I have it illegitimately, then take it back." He held forth the staff.

Tybalt laughed. "And you actually believe you are doing the honorable thing, you utter fool! *That's* why it honors you, and why I can't just take it. Neither one of you knows any better."

The King was obviously infinitely more powerful than Benny or the staff, but his attitude was becoming annoying. "What the hell do you know about honor? You're just a thoughtless destroyer."

"What do I care about honor?" Tybalt asked rhetorically. "I have power, which is far better. But I want my staff back, and I have to make a deal you find legitimate to recover it from you. Name your terms."

"What good would any terms be, if you destroy the world I must live in?"

"You seek to debate me, you microscopic pipsqueak?" the king demanded wrathfully. "Then I will simply have to abolish you along with your world, even if it means the loss of the staff." He lifted the fireball, which started to expand ominously.

Then an even larger figure appeared behind Tybalt. A hand swung down and knocked the king to the ground as if he were a feeble insect. He landed on his back, surprise transforming to rage as his fireball fell from his hand and guttered out. "Who dares?" he demanded.

"As if it were your province to question me," the figure said, kneeling so that the whole of her came into view. It was a woman in a shining robe, ethereally lovely.

"Sethrida!" Tybalt exclaimed, sitting up. "Appointed by the Lord!"

"That is the meaning of my name," she agreed. "I come to recover my Horns." She lifted her other hand, which held the two broken Horns. She set them on her head above her ears, where they merged immediately with the flesh and became whole again. They were part of her!

Benny stared. He could not do otherwise. He would have thought that horns would make a woman look like a devil, but these only enhanced her beauty. She had been sent by the Protector?

The king recovered his bluster. "It is too late for you to interfere, Sentinel," he said. "We Titans have been summoned, and now it is our right and duty to destroy this world. Even you cannot deny us." He formed another fireball, which quickly grew larger than the first. "Now depart, spooky spirit, and leave us to our endeavor. You have recovered your horns and have no further business here."

"You forget that the Horns have been neutralized," Sethrida said. "Your summoning has been revoked. This world is not yours to play with."

"So you say," Tybalt said. "But I will not deny my minions their pleasure at this stage. Get you gone."

"I regret the need to discipline you," the Sentinel murmured. "But you have become annoyingly willful."

"And what are you going to do about it, female?" His tone was increasingly ugly.

"Nothing. Your own unbridled passion will destroy you."

"Oh?" the King said ironically. The fireball in his hand continued to grow. "Maybe after this flame consumes you, wench."

Sethrida merely gazed at him. The king, still sitting, threw the fireball at her.

It did not fly. It remained attached to his hand, still growing. Surprised, he tried again, and failed again, as Benny and the Sentinel watched.

The fire expanded to encompass Tybalt's hand. Now pain showed on his face. His own fire was consuming him! It traveled along his arm, then took in his body, engulfing him in flame. He did not even have time to scream before his body was burned to ash.

The Sentinel blew, and the ash dissipated into the air in a thinning cloud. Then she faced Benny. "I regret you had to witness that," she said. "I tried to persuade him to depart in peace, but his soul was corrupted by his supposed power and it had to be done. Now I believe his minions will depart without further disruption."

Indeed, the other Sky Titans had returned to form a circle around her as the Sentinel stood, towering over them. She made a small gesture with one hand, as of flicking off dust, and they quickly retreated. They had gotten the message.

Benny suspected that he should keep his mouth shut, but his mouth did not cooperate. "Couldn't there have been a better way to make the point than killing him?"

"Kill him?" she asked blankly.

"Burning him up like that."

She smiled, and it was like the sun emerging from a dark cloud. "Ah, now I see. The Titans are immortal. What you saw was not killing but banishing; his fabricated local host was incinerated, sending him back to his home plane. It will be a while before he travels again to another planet."

Oh. A special effect. "Uh, thanks," Benny said. "Does this mean that our word of Pakk will survive?"

"It does. The Protector has not yet slated this particular world for extinction. The Titans were supposed to merely chasten it, not eliminate it, so I came to rectify the error."

Not *yet* slated? That made Benny nervous. "We're still on probation?"

"Yes. We hope it will not be necessary to wipe the slate clean and start over. That would cost a few millennia and be inefficient. We do not enjoy inefficiency."

Benny gazed at her, assimilating that. "I hope we can become more efficient."

She smiled again. "Come up here, if we are to converse."

"Uh, okay. But how?"

She put a hand down, and Benny sat on her palm, holding on to her thumb, which was about a foot and a half long yet marvelously slender and contoured, like her body. Her robe was vague in the manner of fog, and as he passed upward he fancied he could see the shapely columns of her thighs, the evocative narrowing of her waist, and the breathtaking outline of her swelling bosom beneath the vapor. She was every foot a woman!

She lifted him up to the level of her face. Her great rainbow eyes focused on him. They were brightly defined in the otherwise somewhat misty expanse of her face, as was her mouth. "Hello, Benny Clout," she murmured. "Have you any other questions?" Her lustrous, dawn-hued hair flared slightly with seeming life of its own as she spoke.

Benny tried to suppress his awe. "Yes, if you have time for them. I don't want to keep you from your more important pursuits."

She laughed, and her breath was like a flower scented summer breeze. "I am attending to them as we speak, Benny. This is not my complete aspect. This part of my attention has all the time you may require."

Oh. "Tybalt told me that my staff is stolen goods. That's why he came to me. I love the staff, but I can't keep it if that's the case."

"That is the case, but not the complete case," she said. "Tybalt himself stole it for his collection. Later it was stolen from him. He has no more right to it than you do."

"But still—"

"It is yours as long as you use it for good. Be satisfied with that. Anything else?"

He plowed on. "Yes. I—I am curious why the Protector should ever have placed your horns there, and why he made the stipulation of using them to summon the Sky Titans to destroy the world, since I gather you don't wish to destroy it at this time. It seems to be to be downright dangerous to leave them there, where any fool like one of us might blow them." Not that Dale was a fool, but he had been tricked into blowing the wrong Horn.

"He did not exactly place them here, Benny," she said. "I have been here all along, reposing beneath the ground where my horns were set, resting until my attention was required. I do not like to stay far from my body parts." The two horns on her head glowed faintly.

"You—that mountain was on your body?"

"That mountain *was* my body, to a fair degree, covered with a blanket of stone and earth. I am larger than I may appear."

"I, uh, see," Benny said awkwardly. "You—you are the Sentinel, but is that all?"

"Hardly. I am what you might think of as the Planet Mother, the spirit in all things. The Sentinel is the aspect that watches for mischief."

"That's why you are so lovely!" Benny exclaimed. "You are Nature. You define perfection."

She smiled. "In a manner. It depends on your perception and comprehension." She paused. "Your friends have returned, and are confused about my form. I can appear smaller, if you prefer." Then her hand shrank, along with her body, until he was deposited back on the ground and she stood before him no taller than he was, still excruciatingly lovely. The horns, now petite, took nothing from her beauty. "Is that better?"

"Uh, any size you want to be is fine with me. I'm just glad to have met you."

"You meet me in all that you see on this world, if you but have the wit to perceive it."

"I will be aware of it the rest of my life," Benny said fervently.

She stepped forward and kissed him. "Thank you."

Then, as he stood stunned, she introduced herself to Dale, Helena, and Burgundy, clarifying her presence. She also explained about the Horns. "They were never meant for destructive purpose. The Protector is above all merciful, and in his mercy he placed the horns there, and me with them as I rested, so that they could be used to aid Pakk, not destroy it. Over the centuries, the true story of the Twin Horns was skewed and misinterpreted through the generations of Pakk's inhabitants. Their original purpose was indeed to summon the Guardians, such as the Sky Titans, but only to destroy the evil in the world. If even one person upheld the goodness, truth, and beauty that was left in Pakk, the hand of the Sky Titans would be stayed. You and your companions selflessly sacrificed your well-being in fighting the Kudgels, and attempting to save a world filled with evil. Your actions could be nothing but that same goodness, truth, and beauty."

"I don't think I am worthy of any such honor," Benny said. "I have been blundering along, making so many mistakes. There are so many things I would change, if I could do them over."

"But you are learning. You ponder your mistakes and try to do better thereafter. That is the truth and beauty of the process. So few mortal humans do." The others nodded.

"But that learning hurts!" Benny protested. "I have lost close friends like Laughing Jack and my wife, Virtue. I know I can't ever replace them in my heart." He was on the verge of breaking down, and he hated that, because he knew he was feeling sorry for himself and wasting Sethrida's time. But he couldn't stop the memories and the anguish. "I feel so lost without them!"

The figure before him shifted and became Laughing Jack. "Buck up and stop complaining," he said gruffly.

Dale chuckled and Helena smiled.

Benny fell back, astonished. Then he realized that the Sentinel had merely assumed Jack's form for the moment. But it helped. "I'll try," he promised.

The figure became Bum, his orc friend. "Don't try. *Do* it."

Now Benny had to smile. "Thanks, friend. But still, Virtue—"

"And as for Virtue," Bum said, "She's not quite as dead as you might think."

"But—"

The figure morphed again. Now it was Virtue. "Oh, Benny!" she exclaimed, running to hug him as the others smiled again.

He had to hug her back, and kiss her. But he knew he was fooling himself. This was the Sentinel assuming her aspect, as Magenta had before. It wasn't real.

She stepped back a pace. Now her form became translucent. "Oh, Benny, I'm fading," she said. "You don't believe in me."

What could he say? "Virtue, I love you! But the witch killed you."

Her form firmed a bit. "Not entirely. I was able to combat her spell somewhat. I saved my spirit by disengaging before my body died. But now I'm much like a ghost, and I know no way to revive myself, or save the life of our unborn daughter."

"Oh, Virtue!" Benny moaned, stricken again.

"I'm sorry, but I must ask. Is Ammarod alive?"

And she still had feelings for the man. Benny hesitated to answer.

"Ammarod is dead," Dale said.

"How did he die? Was there any way to spare him?"

"I killed him," Benny said. "We were in combat. I absorbed part of him."

The Sentinel reappeared. "Benny tried to spare Ammarod," she said. "But he would not accept Benny's forgiveness and help. He was far too manipulated by Winona to change, though he wanted to. Now he is part of Benny, who may, in time, discover how to use his properties and memories."

Virtue reappeared. "I—I have to say I am relieved. Ammarod was no longer the man I had known. I wish there had been some way for me to make peace with him."

Sethrida reappeared. "The Protector gave me the option and power of restoring Ammarod as well as Winona, but I feel that this would not be a good idea. In an imperfect world like Pakk, they could revert to their evil ways. However, in the Afterlife, through the Protector's mercy, they and others like them may indeed redeem themselves, and the Protector may still have good work for them, as he has for Dale. It is not known for sure at this time, but the possibility exists. It all depends on them."

"And there's still a chance for me to know my mother other than as an antagonist?" Benny asked. "As well as for Virtue to make peace with Ammarod?"

"Not on this world or in this life, but in the hereafter, in another time and place. At present we must settle things for Virtue."

Virtue returned. "I must leave you," she said sadly. "This is not my body. But I will always be with you in spirit." She faded, and Sethrida reappeared.

Benny, distraught, suffered a pang of anger. "Why are you teasing me, Sentinel?" he demanded. "If you can't make Virtue whole again, why flash her before me like this?"

"I *can* revive her completely," Sethrida said seriously. "But her physical time in Pakk is over. The Protector needs her on other worlds, just as one day you and Dale and Helena will be needed on other worlds. It is better not to meddle further, lest there be unfortunate complications."

She could bring Virtue back? He was tempted to beg her to do that, but knew that any complications that made the force of Nature hesitate were bound to overwhelm him. Yet maybe there was something to be salvaged. "Our child—what about her? She can't just appear on some other world as a baby."

Sethrida considered briefly. "True. That much is feasible. She can be here, if there is a woman willing to carry her."

"I'll do it," Helena offered.

The Sentinel looked at her. "No. You are already with child, a boy."

"A boy!" Dale exclaimed, ecstatic.

Benny was glad for them, but sorry that this meant there was no host for his daughter. Damn!

"She is here," Sethrida said. Benny wasn't sure whom she meant.

Magenta materialized before them, having completed her teleportation. She looked about, startled. "Who are you?"

"Let me touch you and you will know," Sethrida said, extending her hand.

Magenta took the hand, and seemed about to faint as she assimilated the woman's nature. "Oh! I somehow thought you'd be larger."

"Like this?" the Sentinel asked, abruptly appearing in her full size.

"Yes," Magenta said, awed.

Sethrida reappeared in human size. "Size is largely irrelevant in the larger scheme. There may be a task for you to do."

Magenta looked at Benny. "I came to help Benny, knowing I have a role to play in his future. But I don't know what it is."

The Sentinel's body became Virtue. "It is to carry my baby, since I can't stay on Pakk in physical form. My body is dead, on this world. I can see how you would not want to do that."

"Of course I'll do it!" Magenta said.

"Are you sure? You would have to marry Benny."

"As if that would be a chore, were he not already committed to you."

"Then here it is," Virtue said. Her belly glowed, becoming an orb of light. She stepped into Magenta, briefly merging with her. Then she stepped out again, no longer glowing.

"Oh!" Magenta repeated. Now the glow was in her, fading.

"Farewell," Virtue said, waving to them all. She looked at Magenta. "Take care of Benny, please."

"I will," Magenta said, clearly taken aback.

Then Virtue was gone, and Sethrida was back. "Benny, your marriage to Virtue is not over, and will never be over. But it is no longer relevant on Pakk. Magenta is now your local wife. She will bear Virtue's child, and the two of you will have more children in the future. That aspect is now in place."

"Uh," Benny said, at a loss for coherent words.

Magenta laughed. "You had *better* marry me. I'm carrying your child. What's her name?"

"Laurel," Benny said before he thought. "After her mother, as she was originally."

"What about yours?" Burgundy asked Helena.

Helena looked at Dale. "Jack Zorn Ducat," he said. "After Laughing Jack, my adoptive brother Zorn, and my father Nolan Ducat."

"Oh," Helena said. "Mona nudged me."

"Who?" Magenta asked.

"Mona. Desdemona Dryad. She animates my pendant." Helena touched the amulet she wore around her neck. "She married Nolan, before she died. This baby is not of her line, but she's romantic. She likes having the baby with us. She's fairly close to him." Indeed, the pendant hung just above her belly.

Sethrida smiled. "It is a good association. Now it is time for the remaining Sky Titans to return to their sky. I must caution them never to bother Pakk again, although other forces will." She made a minor gesture, and the circle of Sky Titans reappeared, looming over them all. "Return to your home in the clouds, and remember your true purpose."

"What is that purpose?" one Titan asked. "We were doing as King Tybalt directed."

"To protect this planet, not despoil it," the Sentinel said. "Tybalt was corrupted, and is no longer your king."

The Sky Titans did not question this. They lifted off the ground, flying into the sky, and were soon gone.

The Sentinel oriented on the remaining group. "My work here is done. Virtue will remain with me for a time. She will bid you farewell."

The form became Virtue. "Oh, Benny!" she said tearfully. She went to him and kissed him once more. Then she hugged each of the others in turn, Dale, Helena, Burgundy, Kolpak, and finally, Magenta, with special passion. "I will visit you when I can," she said.

Which meant that Benny would get to see her again, on occasion, and perhaps hold her. That notion was precious.

Virtue stepped back and became Sethrida, who lifted a hand in parting and faded out.

They stood in numb silence for a moment. Then Dale spoke. "We must honor our dead before we go."

They held a small ceremony for the dead, including Quill. Then they bid farewell also to Kolpak, who faced the sad chore of trying to organize the remaining frost dwarves to rebuild Alfen Gulfadex. There was work to be done all across the planet. Benny had invited Burgundy the dwarf to stay in Gant for a while, but the dwarf had other business in tracking down his former master, the wizard.

"One thing, Burgundy," Dale said. Benny was surprised because Dale seldom, if ever, called the dwarf by his name. What was on his mind?

The dwarf was surprised too. "What?"

"I have a favor to ask."

Now they were all curious. What could it be?

"Um," Burgundy said noncommittally.

"My mother, the water spirit, is in this flask," Dale said, holding it up. "The Kudgels poisoned the water of her pool. I was hoping the wizard could purify her so she won't die, and return her to safe water. But we never saw the wizard. I can't bear the thought of her dying like this. Now, if you find him—"

Burgundy didn't hesitate. He was clearly pleased and honored to be given a mission of this importance. "Yes, of course. I will guard it with my life." He took the flask and put it carefully in his pack.

It was time for them to go home.

✦

It was time for the festival of the winter solstice, which consisted mainly of feasting, and the Fox Den was preparing for a celebrating throng. Dale, Bum, and Liverwart were there, and of course Helena and Magenta, both obviously pregnant.

There was the sound of horses outside. Benny and the others went out to meet the visitors.

It was Nadia, the former barmaid, along with a scrawny man with curly blond hair. It was Benny's older brother Aiken!

"That's who Nadia left me for," Dale said darkly.

"The bastard!" Benny exclaimed, and punched his brother hard in the face. The days when Aiken had pushed him around were long gone; Benny was now bigger and stronger. Aiken dropped to the ground.

"No!" Nadia screamed.

But Benny had more of a score to settle. He aimed a kick at the fallen man.

Dale caught him from behind and heaved him off the ground. "Don't be so quick to kill your other brother, too!"

"How can you forgive Aiken for abandoning me, and Nadia for leaving you?" Benny demanded.

Dale smiled as he carefully set Benny back on the ground, alert lest he renew his attack. "Virtue taught me forgiveness," he said. "I have profited much by it. Remember, it even won Helena for me, on your suggestion. It truly can be better to forgive than to fight. Nadia and I weren't right together and we knew it. I am happy for Aiken and Nadia because they learned to love just as I did. They are right for each other. You should be happy too."

Benny knew he was right, but couldn't make himself say so yet. He stood there, chewing his lip.

Aiken got up and approached, his hands spread. "Benny, I am so sorry for the way I treated you when we were youths," he said. "I was never there for you. Far from it! I tried to drown my inadequacy in drink. But I can say for myself that I was not a complete loss. Winona came to me several times in my drunkenness and asked me to join her, but at least I had the gumption to refuse. I was a failure in life, but she would have made me evil. Then, at last, I connected with Nadia, and she got me off the drink and made a man of me." He looked at her with open love.

"I knew too well what chronic drunkenness could lead to," Nadia said. "I saw it every day at the tavern. But Laughing Jack told me of an herb that could help, if a man really wanted to be helped, and I gave it to Aiken."

Aiken had refused Winona's blandishments even when drunk? There had indeed been a core of decency in him.

"Is there anything I can do, any possible way to make it up to you?" Aiken asked. "I want so much for it to be right between us."

How could Benny hold a grudge against that? He was wrong to condemn the man, when so much had changed. "Just be the brother you should have been," he said shortly.

Aiken hugged him. Benny wasn't actually too keen on that, but again, how could he refuse?

Then Nadia hugged him too, something he would have loved before he met Virtue. "Thank you for being so generous," she said.

Generous? This was embarrassing. They were giving him far more credit than he deserved.

"Baby Laurel kicked me as you and Aiken embraced," Magenta murmured. "I think she approves."

"So does Mona," Helena said, touching her pendant. "She loves it when families reunite."

"I must travel," Dale said. "But I think the journey is too arduous for you in your present condition. Stay with Benny while I'm gone."

"Where are you going?" Helena asked him, surprised.

He lifted his own ash pendant, which she had given him. "I just got the urgent word, and it is not to be denied. I must visit a stubborn old man named Nolan Ducat. I hear he has a little girl dying to meet her half-brother."

Helena laughed. "It's about time. Give them my greeting."

"We'll take care of you," Benny agreed, and Magenta nodded.

"One other thing, just in case," Dale said. "Benny, remember long ago when Cycleze gave you a map that identifies where I buried much of my wealth?"

"I put it safely away," Benny said. "I never really looked at it. I was never after wealth, yours or anyone else's."

"Now I think you should use it to locate and take that wealth to rebuild and renovate Gant and the Fox Den. It can do everyone some good, and maybe make a place in the Gant River where my mother the water spirit can live safely, when Burgundy finds the wizard and saves her."

Oh. "Of course," Benny agreed. He wondered why this had come up at this moment. Then he saw Helena touch her ash pendant, and realized that the tree spirit wanted to help the water spirit. It did make sense. It would be wonderful to have them both in the vicinity, part of the larger family.

Epilogue

"And now, thanks to your unrelenting investigation into my personal life, it's morning and I haven't gotten a wink of sleep." Pawben pointed at the window by the staircase, the first tree-filtered rays of sun illuminating the floor.

"Wow, you're right Ben. I was so caught up in your tale I didn't even notice. You're going to be slap-ass tired for your trip home," the tortoise said.

Pawben laughed and snapped his fingers, and then pointed back to the window. Toadstool was shocked to see it was once again night time. "Maybe the powers at hand will now let me get a good eight hours without sending me off to meet another dearly departed loved one."

"Thank you for sharing the story, Ben. I know it must be hard to share so many bad memories."

"They're not bad...not all of them at least. Although I agree this tale was perhaps one of the most traumatic, to lose so much so soon in life."

"Well, what was all that the Sentinel said about possibly reuniting with your family on other worlds? I know you were a world jumper before retiring to our world, but did you make amends with your mother and brother like you'd hoped?" Toadstool asked.

The Pawben was moved by the question, and the tortoise quickly regretted his asking when he saw tears well up in the old human's eyes. But there was some joy in the sadness.

"I have had no interaction with my mother or her spirit, although I still hold out hope for some form of amendment…"

Toadstool leaned forward "And Ammarod?"

Pawben smiled, "He and I did manage to help each other in our missions on other worlds, in a manner of speaking. You could say we made peace with each other."

"Maybe one day you'll share the details?" The tortoise tried to shield his question as more of a rhetorical statement, but it didn't work for the Pawben.

"I dunno…certainly not now." Pawben stood again and looked over at the small boy sleeping peacefully on the other end of the room and his heart filled with sorrow. "And then there's the memory of what happened to my dear friend Dale Beranger, and his son…"

Toadstool sat silently as the old, bearded man and his staff descended the stairs. "You've always seemed to skirt over that tale, too," he whispered to himself rather than Pawben.

"My fist is gonna *skirt* across your face if you don't hush and let me sleep," Pawben yelled from the couch downstairs.

Toadstool was shocked at first when he realized his friend had heard his whisper from downstairs and then smiled. His friend was, after all, the Pawben. So Toadstool walked over to his own bed and crawled under the covers beside Aldwin, knowing full well the Pawben wouldn't be able to resist weaving another tale for them over a mid-day picnic the next day.

"Don't count on it!" the Pawben yelled.

But Toadstool is right, Pawben thought. He would indeed share more stories with him and Aldwin…and wait for whatever and whenever that final adventure Virtue had spoken of would occur. He couldn't stand the thought of another adventure now, but knew deep down he looked forward to helping Aldwin Beranger grow into the young man his father and grandfather had hoped for. He wished

Dale, Helena, and countless other companions could somehow make this journey with him. In his old age, he felt vulnerable again, as he did in those early years with Beranger and Cycleze. They would watch over him, though, as the Protector would, in their preferred way and not his.

Author's Note:
Piers Anthony

As with the prior novels of this trilogy, Kenneth Kelly started it and I finished it, at least the main text. The middle is mixed.

At this writing I am 82 years old, and have been married for 60 years. I fear that any decade now I will start to feel my age. For example, when I edited this novel I found that we were using different conventions for indenting paragraphs. Ken used tabs, while I had the automatic indent. To get a uniform format I needed to eliminate his tabs, but that was tedious. I could have done it in one step by using a macro, but my Linux LibreOffice word processor over the years has made it harder and harder to have macros, and with the current version I don't have them at all. What programmers have against macros I don't know, but short of hiring one to put them back in, I'm stuck. So I tried Find and Exchange, but my Find command can't identify the tabs. Surely a geek—that is, computer expert—could do it, but I'm just an ordinary user, and in my dotage I can't figure it out. So I had to do it all "by hand," consuming frustrating time. The programmers must be laughing. But I do feel old.

However, the work on the novel itself was another matter. I pride myself on having more imagination than most other writers I see, but I hardly had to draw on it this time. Ken had the chapters so thoroughly worked out that all I had to do was fill out the details and amplify where necessary. Often in my individual novels I reach a point where I realize I have the beginning, ending, and a general idea of the whole, but need inspiration to fill in several tens of thousands of words of the middle. In school and college we called it mid semester slump; it happens in novels too. That was no problem here; I simply followed his outline.

This novel concludes the trilogy. I have other projects to move on to, but it hardly seems likely that the series will end here. Ken's mind is already percolating on drastic new developments.

Readers who want to know more of me can find me at my web site, www.HiPiers.com, where I run a monthly blog-type column calculated to aggravate anyone with any reasonable wit, and an ongoing survey of electronic publishers and related services, with no holds barred feedback on good and bad publishers, intended to assist writers who have dreams without publishers. As I have said before, I remember how it was; from the time I made my decision to be a professional writer, it took me a college BA in creative writing and eight years to make my first sale. When I fought to get an honest accounting from my first novel publisher, instead I got blacklisted for six years. I'm not sure it's easier now, and time has not mellowed me much. The main difference is that today I can expose bad publishers without much fear of retaliation, because they know that today I have the will and the means to take it to them if they try. Few do.

Magenta Salvation was proofread by Scott M. Ryan and Anne White.

Now get on to the next Author Note to meet Ken Kelly.

Author's note:
Ken Kelly

This year has been a rough one for me. Due to circumstances I won't elaborate on here, my life has been completely turned upside down. I was forced to temporarily stop graduate school, lost my job, and have been dealing with depression and other issues for most of 2016. People I thought were friends abandoned me, and I had to completely start over in every aspect of my life. Thus, the tone of this book is somewhat darker than the previous installments. Benny has lost everything: Laughing Jack, Virtue, along with the terrible revelation of his mother and half-brother. He has been separated and seemingly abandoned by his companions, all with the fate of Pakk hanging over his head. There is no light at the end of his tunnel, just as there seemed to be no light at the end of mine. His despair caused him to act out in ways unbefitting of his character, such as getting drunk and killing Belasco and his companions. Much like my despair caused me to act in ways I normally didn't.

However, as bad as things seemed and still seem, this cloud still has a silver lining. Piers Anthony stuck by me when many others didn't. He could've very easily told me to hit the road when my drama started, but he didn't. He didn't sugar coat things, or coddle me for my mistakes, but he showed compassion and concern. Piers saw past my flaws and helped my writing become something it never could have been otherwise. I have a long way to go before my life returns to normal, but the Pakk books I've written with Piers Anthony have been a blessing in my life that has helped me cling to the cliff's edge. I don't expect to become rich and famous off these books, although I won't complain if I do. But mostly, I hope my writing can have some type of impact on the reader; that they can take something away besides an entertaining story. Hopefully, the reader hasn't seen the last of Benny Clout. Perhaps Piers and I can work together on future projects if deemed feasible. Regardless of what the future holds, though, you definitely haven't seen the last of Benny Clout. I sound like a broken record, but this wouldn't have been possible without Piers Anthony. Thus, I'll end this author's note with a quote from this very book: as Nolan Ducat said of his son Dale, when Piers Anthony needs me I'll be there.